Praise for Tamsen Parker and Craving Flight

"Very, very much worth reading. It's satisfying and compelling and emotionally rich in both the emotional sense, but also in a cultural, almost world-building sense."

—*Smart Bitches Trashy Books*

"Different, vibrant and respectful of the Orthodox Jewish culture and also deeply sexy."

—*Dear Author*

"So much more than just an erotic BDSM romance […] fascinating and sweet."

—*Smexy Books*

"A thought provoking and intense erotic romance."

—*Heroes and Heartbreakers*

"Intense, erotic and full of heart. A perfect mix of raw passion and tenderness makes Craving Flight irresistible."

—*Kit Rocha, New York Times Bestselling Author of the Beyond Series*

"Tamsen Parker wrote an accurate depiction of extremely orthodox religious life and incorporated it into an unorthodox lifestyle. She did it beautifully and passionately and it shows—in the descriptions, the terminology and the delicate way the interpersonal relationships in this culture are written."

—*The Book Hammock*

"If you want hot, engaging, realistic and dirrrrrty BDSM romance, Tamsen Parker is your woman. [...] Lovely, hot and well-crafted."

—*Alyssa Cole, Author of Radio Silence*

"Thoughtful, complex, and erotic."

—*Darlene's Digest*

CRAVING FLIGHT

TAMSEN PARKER

For Coco,
Happy reading*
Happy reading*
thanks for coming
to NECRWA16!
xoxo
Tamsen

Craving Flight: © 2015 by Tamsen Parker

Cover Design by Amber Shah of Book Beautiful
(www.bookbeautiful.com)

Print Edition

For M, who has supported my outlandish ideas from the beginning. You have only yourself to blame.

Table of Contents

Foreword

This novella is a product of the *Bring Out Your Kink ~ Bound by Ink* writing event sponsored by the Goodreads BDSM Group. Members provided a photo and letter to inspire writers to create an original story. Writers picked the prompt that spoke to them most. A written description of the image that inspired this story is provided below along with the original request letter.

A woman in profile, eyes cast down. Clearly holding the camera at arm's length, she wears a long-sleeved, olive-green shirt that covers up to the hollow of her throat, a black pearl necklace and drop earrings. Her hair is covered by intricately tied scarves of blue, grey, bronze and gold, the interwoven tail is draped over her shoulder. She is at once modest and on display.

Dear pervert,

I am a deeply modest yet profoundly kinky woman. My husband left me for another woman, so I divorced him. During our marriage, I discovered that I had a need for restraint, spanking during sex play, and some rather kinky drives. He was my husband but resisted being my Dom though he agreed to "play" sometimes during sex.

My bed proclivities represent only one area where I

have grown and evolved. I also have become more modest as I have grown older. I cover my arms to the elbow, my legs to the knee, and my collar bones. While not frumpy, I chose to dress to save my charms for the next and only master I will have. Also I have long auburn hair that I keep tightly bound and covered with beautiful scarves called tichels…keeping that part of myself hidden for my next master. My hair hasn't been seen by a man since I last was with my husband five years ago.

I am a sexual submissive that is dominant in other life roles (career, academic, etc.). While my ex-husband did try at times to meet my needs, I have craved a master who would demand my full submission…perhaps one who would demand a much deeper power exchange and much more intensive exploration of pain play…allowing impact, bondage, violet wand, clamping, wax, and pain but no edge or fluid play.

Please…I beg you to unwind my scarves, take down my hair, bind me in the literal and figurative ropes of your dominion with shibari and pain, so that I may finally fly free.

Please,
Craving Flight

PROLOGUE

"**G**OOD AFTERNOON, TZIPPORAH."
"Good afternoon, Elan."

His jaw tightens at my response, only barely visible by the shift of his beard. I have to resist swallowing. His eyes focus on my mouth, my lips, and then his gaze travels down my neck to the buttoned-up collar of my shirt. The wings inside me beat harder under his gaze. Even though it makes me nervous because his dark eyes are so intense, I don't truly mind his scrutiny. I like the way he looks at me.

With the shop being relatively empty and his attention distracted by examining what I'm wearing, it gives me a chance to return the favor and study him. The way his broad shoulders fill out his white shirt, how the fabric grazes his biceps. But his forearms…those are definitely my favorite. The sleeves rolled up nearly to his elbows show off the veins and muscles, the masculine dusting of hair that reaches to his wrists. His hands—battered and scarred from his work but scrubbed clean—rest on the counter behind the glass. I even admire his clipped-to-the-quick fingernails.

"What can I get for you today?" His words startle me. How much longer have I been staring at him than he's been staring at me? Blood rushes to my cheeks and my face grows hot. Forget my cheeks. I must be blushing from my collar to the tichels that cover my head. It's a ridiculous thought, but I'm so flustered, I think my hair might even be turning redder under the scarves. My reactions to even the most innocent interactions with Elan are visceral. It's as though he knows how to communicate with the very center of me.

"Half a pound of ground beef, please."

His expression doesn't change, implacable as ever, but there's a small shake of his head. I'm confident he finds me faintly ridiculous. This interloper who hasn't quite adapted to her new surroundings. I stick out like a parrot in the taiga. I'm trying, have been trying, but I don't know that I'll ever feel completely at home here.

"Spaghetti and meatballs again?" Am I imagining the tinge of judgment in his voice? I could be. I've been told I'm overly sensitive to these things. Probably the result of too much of my life spent studying other people, watching for nuances, coding and decoding the words they've said and trying to figure out *What does it all mean?* Four years as an undergraduate, six years earning a PhD, nine more as a professor teaching classes and doing research, and I haven't figured it out yet.

His hands come off the counter and he tears a piece of waxed paper from a large roll before he pulls on gloves and takes a tray from behind the spotless glass of the case. Something else I like about Elan: how easily he moves in his work, how at home he is here. We have that in common—competence in our occupations, though his is with his hands and mine is mostly in my mind. He weighs the meat and hands me a package tied with care along with some counsel. "Don't forget, no Parmesan cheese."

"Yes, I know."

It's kindly meant, I think, but it mortifies me. I've been keeping kosher since I moved to this neighborhood in Brooklyn. It should be second-nature after so long but even now I make mistakes. He gives me reminders sometimes because he knows I can be forgetful.

It's such a cliché, the absent-minded professor, but I've been that way my whole life. Always with my nose stuck in a book, my brain churning with abstract thoughts instead of paying attention to worldly things. I've gotten caught out in the rain with my laptop before because I didn't notice the gathering clouds, and if I want to have a hope of being on time for anything I need to set alarms. I've gotten better at hiding exactly how scatterbrained I am and it embarrasses me that he knows.

Our fingers nearly brush as I take the small parcel and the almost-contact is electric. At least for me it is.

"Thank you," I murmur, tucking the meat into my grocery bag that already holds a box of pasta, and vegetables to make the sauce. Tomatoes, zucchini, and onions I'll chop carefully in my quiet apartment and put on the stove to simmer while I grade the papers I collected during the seminar I just taught. I have high hopes since they're my seniors and it's October, but I don't like to count on anything. We'll see.

"You're welcome, Tzipporah." The sound of my name formed by his mouth, the breath he expended to say it, to acknowledge me, sends a pleasurable chill up my spine that I try to ignore as I pay the younger man at the register.

Turning to leave, I feel Elan's eyes on me as I go. What is he thinking as he watches the gentle sway of my skirt around my calves, the tightly wrapped colorful silk that crowns my head, the press of my palm to the door as I push it open to head out to the sidewalk? Or am I inventing the weight of his attention? I don't turn around to find out.

I think of him as I walk down the street; the work of his strong hands safe in the sack that hangs from my shoulder, his soft but compelling voice, his presence behind the counter as reliable as the sun. He's always there.

Though I've tried to ignore it and would never admit it to anyone, I've had a certain fascination with Elan since I walked into his butcher shop five years ago. And next week, I will become his wife.

CHAPTER ONE

Two Months Earlier

THE TEA I'M holding is hot and outside it's a sticky-August eighty degrees but my hands feel cold. Bina, on the other hand, looks like she's got sunshine streaming out of various orifices. She's practically bouncing in her seat. "Is this about what I think it's about?"

I shouldn't roll my eyes because she's always so kind to me. I know it's her job as the rabbi's wife to be nice to new people but she's taken a special interest in me, and we've become close over the past few years as I've tried to integrate myself into Forest Park and the shul her husband leads. I really shouldn't roll my eyes. And yet. "Probably."

"Well, you *have* been living here for over a year, you know. And coming to the shul for five."

"Oh, I know."

After I divorced Brooks five years ago, I decided to seriously pursue the Orthodox life that had been calling to me since I was a teenager. I started out slowly, researching neighborhoods and taking classes at the outreach center, gradually spending more weekends here so that I could observe Shabbos. After I finished my year at seminary, I took the plunge and moved.

Barely a single day has gone by since then that I haven't had at least one person ask when I was going to find a husband. At thirty-seven, I'm completely over the hill in this community and they desperately want me to adhere to the social norms. Get married, have babies. I'm late, but better late than never.

I've tried to shrug them off, saying I wasn't ready, but at my age, the bubbes won't take that for an answer. They have zero shame about reminding me exactly how loudly my biological clock is ticking. Some of them have tried to foist grandsons, nephews, distant relatives on me. Some of them hadn't offered up any male sacrifices though. Whenever that happens, it's half-insult, half-relief, knowing it's because I'm a ba'alat teshuva, an outsider. Someone who was technically born Jewish but is only now becoming observant. Sure, to people who don't know any better I look and talk like an Orthodox Jew, but even children here can tell I'm a relative newcomer. It's an odd space to occupy.

Bina taps her tea cup with long, manicured fingernails, the hair of her wig brushing her shoulders. If you didn't know she was wearing a sheitel, you'd never be able to tell. She always looks impeccable. And now so very eager. "Well?"

I take a deep breath and blow it out my nose. "I think I'm ready to start looking for a husband."

She claps her hands and squeals. At least this is making someone happy. "I think that's an excellent idea. I've been thinking of matches for you since you rented your apartment. To be honest, even before that."

Yes, I know. The teachers had cautioned us against dating while I was at seminary and I was one of the few people who'd faithfully adhered to the edict. I had too much to accomplish in that year that I didn't want derailed by a relationship. Leave it to me to go back to school while on sabbatical from my professorship.

I'd also shied away from men because I'd been raw from the end of my marriage. I suppose that's what happens when your husband is confused and disgusted by everything that's become important to you.

I still feel as though I'm settling in to the community but it's time. And maybe having yet another tie will help my roots go even deeper. It'll probably convince a few of the people who continue to be skeptical that I'm in this for good.

Bina digs a notebook out of her bag and cracks it open to a tabbed page. There look to be a dozen names on it already, not to mention several that have already been crossed out.

"Bina!"

"What?" She shrugs, a poor imitation of guilt turning down the corners of her mouth. "No harm in *thinking* about it."

This time I do refrain from rolling my eyes because I really am thankful and her attention makes me feel loved and flattered. She's had faith in my commitment, in me, since the beginning. She's been one of the forces keeping me going even though it's been hard. "Fine. What have you got?"

"Avraham Rifkin."

"No! He's a baby."

"He's twenty-two," she protests. "And from a good family."

I shake my head. "They have to be older than my students."

"So picky." And there go half the names on the list, stricken with her vicious pen. "Shmuel Greenbaum?"

"I know I said older than my students, but he doesn't have to be old enough to be my father."

She tsks at me as she removes Mr. Greenbaum from her catalogue of potential suitors. He's a very sweet man, the kind who always keeps hard candies in his pocket, but no. Just, no. "You're never going to find a husband this way. Not here anyway."

Now she's playing hardball. She knows I want to stay in Forest Park. After things ended with Brooks and I'd been on my own, I started my search for the perfect community. I had several criteria: one, it needed to be a reasonable commute from the university where I work. I didn't want to leave my job at Hudson because professorships are few and far between and I'd been dazzlingly lucky to get a tenure-track position as young as I had. I have no intention of starting over at some other university. Two, I wanted it to be Orthodox, but not insanely conservative. It's a tricky space on the continuum, that tipping point between modern Orthodox and Orthodox.

Three, I had to be able to afford it. And four, I wanted someplace that was pretty welcoming to BTs. Not everywhere is so encouraging of ba'alei teshuva.

Forest Park was one of the few neighborhoods that had fit the bill. I'm not interested in shipping off to LA or Israel or even New Jersey to find a match and Bina knows it.

She taps at another name on the list. "What about Levi Hollander?"

If I hadn't just declined a bunch of her suggestions, I'd likely outright refuse. I know who Levi is. I've seen him at various Shabbos dinners, events at the shul, and around the neighborhood. He's also a BT like me. While I'm sure he's very nice, he's perhaps too nice. He's lacking that commanding edge I crave in a man, the very thing Brooks couldn't provide for me. Plus Levi's built a little too much like an insect: thin and angular with slightly bulging eyes. I don't find him attractive. But I refrain from wrinkling my nose and instead hand her a small victory. "Maybe."

"We'll think about him, okay? Going on a date wouldn't hurt anything."

Except that I know how seriously dating is taken here. If I go out with someone, the whole shul will have us halfway to married by the time we're finishing our appetizers.

She names a few more men and I cast votes of yay or nay and finally there's one last name.

"Don't say no to this one right away, all right? He's maybe a strange choice for you, but you should give him a chance at least. For me."

"I will give him due consideration, cross my heart." I mean it, but inside I'm pleading, *please don't say Ephraim Goldmintz. He's exceedingly loud, laughs like a donkey, and smells vaguely of fish.*

"Elan Klein."

"The butcher?"

"Yes, he's a butcher, but you know he was in yeshiva until his father had a stroke. Elan left to run the family business. And he's maybe a little…" Her eyes skate over me and I know what she sees: small-boned, delicate and petite. "…big."

It's true that Elan dwarfs me. He must be a good six feet tall and he's not a beanpole. More like a brick wall. Does she think that's a turn-off? On the contrary. In fact, I've been aware of him since I got here because he does have that particular brand of authority Levi lacks. One that makes me think he might have it in him to—I can't think about that. No sense in raising those hopes at all.

As for being a butcher…that doesn't bother me either. I've been married to someone who was another college professor—met him in fact because he was my dissertation advisor—and I don't need to do it again. Would maybe prefer not to. Having two people in a marriage who live so much in their minds can make for a disengaged partnership. Or it had for Brooks and me.

Intelligence does matter to me though, but like she's said, he's educated, and it takes not a small amount of brains to run a business. "His job doesn't bother me."

Her eyebrows go up and I can see the meddling wheels start to turn in her head now that she knows he's a real candidate. "He's a widower, you know."

I shrug. I'm divorced. That's far more likely to cause issues. "I know. His wife's name was Rivka, right? I met her a few times at the shul, saw her in their shop. She was kind to me."

I have memories of a sturdy, round-faced woman who wore a wig instead of tichels like I do. Always with a greeting and a smile, telling me I should eat more. She treated me as if I belonged here, not like some of the other women who've lived here and been Orthodox their whole lives. Frum from birth, or FFBs, they call people who've grown up Orthodox; observant since their first breath in this world.

Rivka passed away almost two years ago. I paid a visit while the family was sitting shiva. It was the only time Klein Brothers Kosher Butcher had been closed when it wasn't the Sabbath or a holiday. I remember it particularly because it was the only time I've ever seen Elan look small. Sitting on a low stool, his whole body seemed to wither in mourning. My heart had gone out to him. He'd obviously loved her very much.

"Rivka was a good woman," Bina agrees before sipping at her tea. "So perhaps we'll start there?"

Elan Klein. Yes, he's promising.

"Do you think he'd be interested in me? You don't think being a divorced BT will be an issue?" The Kleins are one of the more conservative families in the neighborhood, although Elan is definitely the most liberal of the bunch. His brothers Moyshe and Dovid wear black hats over their kippahs while he wears only the yarmulke, and their full beards contrast with Elan's neatly trimmed one. His mother in particular is one of the people here who isn't particularly warm to BTs and tends to avoid me. But those may not be my biggest problems. "I'm also pretty sure he thinks I'm an idiot."

Bina's head tips in confusion but then recollection lights her face. "Oh, yes. The brisket incident."

My face heats with the hideously embarrassing memory. It was the day I first moved here and I'd been so thrilled to be in my own apartment with my very own kosher kitchen that I'd bought a brisket at the butcher and spent the hours it took to roast salivating over the smell. Only to realize when I sat down to eat that I'd used non-kosher chili powder and had to start all over again. I'd rushed—in tears—back to the shop where Elan was closing up, and had to confess why I was back so soon. He'd sent me home with chicken breasts and told me to try the brisket again the next day. Not unkindly, but still.

Ugh.

I'm half-tempted to ask if all of Forest Park knows about said incident, and if it's gone down in the annals of community lore, but I don't want to know. It was over a year ago. I should try to let it go. But the brand of humiliation in my brain glows again at the memory.

"I doubt it. Everyone makes mistakes."

Not like that. But I let her confident assurance soothe me, covering my embarrassment with more conversation.

"I didn't even know he was looking."

Surely I would've heard. And surely I would've paid attention. Elan is a bit surly, perhaps, but not in a rude way. Just gruff, coarse, with his hard-working hands—my grip tightens on my mug when I think of what he might look like somewhere other than behind his counter, free of his apron and the strictures of the interactions between men and women who aren't related. My mind starts to wander further afield and I follow. I haven't thought of a flesh-and-blood man like this in a long time.

"Looking is maybe a strong word—"

"Bina!"

"Well, he should be. And I can be quite…persuasive."

Just what I need. Bina trying to foist me on some poor unsuspecting man who may still be mourning his wife's death. I'm tempted to thunk my head on the café table but I refrain. What's the worst that could happen? He'll say no. At least it won't be years before we figure out we're wrong for each other, not like with Brooks.

"Fine."

Though she tries to smother it, the smile breaks over her face, and she circles his name with her pen. I'm half-expecting her to start sketching hearts and wedding cakes. She's probably trying to decide which caterer we should use for our reception, imagining what our babies would look like. "I'll see what I can do."

AND THAT IS how I find myself accepting the least romantic proposal in the history of the world a month later. I've been on four dates with Elan in the time intervening, along with seeing him at community events where Bina shoves us together. September is heavy on the Jewish holidays so there have been lots. We've discussed all the important things:

Children? Yes.

Keeping strictly kosher? Yes. Though I'd wrung my hands in my napkin under the table when confessing that despite my best efforts and intentions, it's something I regularly fail at. Not because I don't care—I do, very much—but because it happens to be an area where my brain fails me. By the tightening of his mouth, he'd remembered Brisketgate. I'd thought that might be the end of it, but he'd asked me for another date when dinner was over.

Shomer Shabbos? Yes, though like keeping kosher, I haven't perfected the practice of being entirely observant of the Sabbath and perhaps never will. But it's not for lack of effort.

Moving to Israel? No. Though a couple of his sisters have and he's visited, we're both rather attached to New York.

Keeping our jobs? I don't want to give mine up, perhaps even after we have a family, and he has no intention of going back to yeshiva even if my job could support us both. Says he prefers working with his hands to arguing all day. He'll leave the studies to his brothers.

And as for the chemistry... I do find him intimidating because he is a sizable man, not to mention somewhat curt, but to be honest, that turns me on. The attraction is undoubtedly there on my end and I suspect it's mutual.

Regardless, it's awkward discussing these important and intimate things with someone I barely know, but in some ways it's a relief. Less risk of falling for someone who makes my mouth water but with whom I don't share anything in common. Or coming to find out we're compatible in the bedroom but I find him morally reprehensible.

Of course, there's no way to see if we're a good fit in bed. Which seems a bit silly, given that neither of us are virgins and sex can be a deal breaker as I well know. But rules are rules and we'll keep them. Especially me. I will not be the wicked, worldly woman leading a good frum man into temptation.

But tucked safe in my own bed, away from any possible accusations, I've fantasized about him, hoping that perhaps the stern, severe demeanor will carry over into the bedroom. While I touched myself, I pictured him taking control of me, imagined what it might feel like to be on my knees at his feet, perhaps with my hands bound behind my back. I can hope. But it's not exactly something you can bring up during these conversations.

Would you perhaps like to hit me? Tie me up? Hurt me? Be quite...forceful?

No. Which is too bad, because that's something I

want almost as badly as to be part of this community, live this life. Since I can't ask, I'm hoping the fantasy will be enough to get me through. It could be, with how Elan looks, his gruff manner. Which is more than I could say for Brooks. At the very least, Elan won't sleep around. Perhaps not out of love for me, but because of his faith. It might be sad, but that has to be good enough.

And after a month during which it's been open season on us both, with prospects seemingly vaulting out of the woodwork, we've been driven together by a fear of what else we might end up with. We are, at least, of a similar age—*Those girls*, Elan had groused last week, *Some of them could be my daughters*—and our personalities aren't oil and water.

For his part, he seems to find me pretty—his eyes hardly leave me when we're together—and for mine, I like that he doesn't try to talk over me. It might be nice if he were a little more verbose but I can work with this.

He does seem to feel I'm a bit…strange, but it appears to be a minor inconvenience, not a deal breaker. A good, handsome, hard-working man who can overlook my status as a new-comer and divorced. And if we marry each other, we can make the constant nagging stop. I'd never pegged myself as a marriage-of-convenience type, but then again I've never been subjected to this level of well-intentioned meddling.

"Would you accept me as your husband, Tzipporah?"

"If you'd be willing to take me as your wife." *Take me.*

A wry smile turns up the corner of his mouth. "It will get the wolves off our backs, yes?"

It's the first hint of humor I've seen from the aloof man, and the comparison of the seemingly frail but shrewd old women to vicious wild beasts is enough to make me laugh.

There's a distinct lack of romance, but perhaps we're both too old and world-weary for these things. Maybe we've been made cynical by our first marriages: me, because even the most promising beginning led to heartbreak and infidelity, and him…I think Elan worshipped Rivka, and the idea of getting that lucky in love twice is laughable. Though if I'm being honest, a hint of passion would help me not feel as though I'm a chore to be done.

If I'm spectacularly lucky, shared values and mutual respect dusted with attraction will someday bloom into something akin to love. And if not…well, I'll have cemented my place in the community I love, the place where I can live a life that is faithful to the beliefs that have become the center of my being. Elan and his family are well-liked and respected here, and perhaps some of that will rub off on me. I can only hope.

WHEN I GET home from what I'm hoping will be the last date I ever have to go on, I call my parents, bracing myself for their disapproval as the phone rings. They'd been disappointed when Brooks and I had gotten divorced. I could've told them how he'd cheated on me, but I hadn't wanted to disparage him. Particularly since he'd made me feel like it was my fault. As if my increasing religiosity and growing need for kink had been the reasons for his perfidy.

I've recovered enough of my self-esteem to realize it was nothing about my behavior that forced him to stray—he could've asked for a divorce instead of sneaking around. I wish he would've. But at the time I'd merely wanted to retreat and lick my wounds. And I really don't want to discuss my sexual preferences with my parents. Like I need to give them any more reasons to think I'm some kind of freak.

"Hi, Zoe."

"Dad…"

"Sorry. Tzipporah." He says my name with disdain and the tension in my shoulders grows. It's been years since I changed it. I wouldn't mind an honest mistake now and then—I was his Zoe for thirty-odd years after all—but he barely makes an effort because he disagrees with my choice.

I'd grown up vaguely aware of being Jewish but it was something that defined me about as much as living in a blue house. It was just something that was true but seemed to have very little impact on my day-to-day existence. When I'd expressed interest in having a bat mitzvah though, my parents had indulged me. My brother and sister had thought it was strange, voluntarily adding work to my school schedule, what with the Hebrew classes and everything else involved. But I'd done it.

My very secular parents hadn't shared an opinion one way or the other when I'd become active in Hillel when I was in college and went on a birthright trip to Israel, maybe believing my seeking to be a phase. But it didn't escape my notice that they'd seemed almost relieved when I fell in love with and married Brooks, the waspiest WASP who'd ever donned seersucker, regardless of the fact that he was my dissertation advisor.

Since my great grandparents came here from Eastern Europe, my family's been following the assimilation model. Perhaps my parents thought marrying a gentile would cement my secular status for good. But it hadn't. I'd felt that missing piece just as keenly after I'd gotten married as I had before—perhaps more so. My parents could ignore the things they didn't see every day and probably didn't think much of it.

The first time they'd seen me in a headscarf though, they'd objected. More and more strenuously as I started dressing modestly, and keeping kosher as best I could under the circumstances. Every step, they'd raised eyebrows and sighed. When I moved here, they accused me of joining a cult. If it weren't for how much stress the frum community places on the importance of family, I might've ceased talking to them years ago. Instead I've persisted through their side-eye and micro-aggressions, their groans and contempt, trying to be a family despite our differences.

Telling them I'm marrying a man I've only been dating for a few weeks won't go over well. It won't matter to them that it makes me happy, and they won't care that Elan is a good match for me, better than I had any right to expect.

Forcing my voice into a falsely chipper tone, I get what should be a happy announcement over with. "I have some good news. I'm getting married."

CHAPTER TWO

OUR WEDDING IS on a Tuesday night, which of course my parents grumble about. *Why can you not get married on a Sunday like normal Jews?*

Bina generously sits next to my mom through the ceremony. She must be the most patient and charming woman alive, but I could hear the thoughts running through my mother's head. *Why do I have to sit on the other side of the room from my husband? Maybe it's a good thing none of our relatives could make it. A wedding on a Tuesday? Zoe's lost her mind.*

And perhaps it's paranoia but I don't think Elan's family was much happier, though for opposite reasons. I'd asked on one of our dates if they'd be okay with him marrying a divorced BT. He'd shrugged. "My brothers have married well enough for the whole family."

I think he meant it as a joke but it had made me self-conscious. Too religious for one set of parents, not enough for the other. Will I never make anyone happy?

Regardless, it's too late to fret. The ceremony is over,

the dull gold metal band on my finger proof that I'm a married woman now. Again, I suppose, although many people have told me Brooks didn't count. Perhaps not, but he certainly had an impact on me and not for the better.

I don't want to think about him right now, though. I should be thinking about Elan. My husband.

We're being shown to the room where we'll spend our first moments alone together. I've always wondered what happened in the yichud, and now I get to find out.

When we've been closed in the small room, I sneak a glance at Elan. He's standing there, taking up so much space. It's not as obvious in his shop where the ceilings are high and there's always a counter between us, but in here, he seems…big.

Between the closeness of the room, the enormity of what I've just done, the heat and weight of my dress, and the stifling disapproval of my parents that I can sense though they're filing into the reception with the other guests, I'm feeling overwhelmed. It doesn't help that I haven't eaten or had anything to drink all day since I was determined to fast.

"Tzipporah." Elan's soft voice calls me out of wherever it was I'd drifted off to. I lift my gaze and find him regarding me, intent. "You look like you're about to faint. Sit down, please."

I let him lead me over to a couch. Some wonderful person has put a plate of fruit and nuts and a large carafe of water with some cups on a side table. He pours me a measure and puts it in my hands, curling my reluctant fingers around the glass. It's been years since a man touched me in a deliberate way and the contact is shocking, creating an intense burst of pleasure that stuns me.

The way Elan treats me is already different than Brooks. Brooks had been hungover at the ceremony and so drunk at the reception I hadn't been sure we'd have a wedding night at all. We had, but it was perfunctory at best before he'd passed out and I'd been awoken in the middle of the night to him heaving into our hotel room toilet. I should've known then.

"Is it really that bad?"

Is that what he thinks? I turn to face him and the furrow between his brows leads me to believe that yes, he's attributing my dazed state to regret.

"No. It's not. You're not…" I struggle to find the words to explain. I'm happy to be married to him, I'm looking forward to starting our life together, but there's a certain finality to this day. I didn't expect to mourn my former life, thought I'd become acclimated to the new one, gotten over how much my day-to-day existence has changed. It doesn't make any sense. I'm happier now than I've ever been, feel more fulfilled, respected and valued. And yet…

He's tipped his head to look at me, that same patient, intent look he always has. Am I going to survive being married to this man who can make me blush and stammer with no more than a look? Will he forever make me feel flustered and out of sorts?

"Please don't think I regret this. I wouldn't have

agreed to marry you if I didn't want to, no matter how much nagging I was subject to." A corner of his mouth tugs up because he knows exactly what I'm talking about. He's been on the receiving end of quite a bit of "encouragement" too. With that small change in his features, I feel lighter. He's not always so severe. "I'm very happy with my choice, but my parents aren't. I'm sorry I'm letting it temper my happiness."

He shrugs and nudges the cup toward my lips. I tip the glass and the water in my mouth is cool. It doesn't quench my thirst though, but whets it, making me swallow the whole glass in a rush. I immediately want more, but he shakes his head. "Have something to eat before you have any more to drink. You don't want to upset your stomach."

I know. It's not like I've never fasted before. I know how to break the fast without getting sick. There are few things more pathetic than a bride puking on her wedding day. Elan already thinks I'm silly, I don't need him thinking I'm a complete and utter moron.

After I've crunched a handful of almonds between my teeth and swallowed, I realize he's watching me instead of eating himself. "You should eat too."

"I will, now that I'm not worried you're going to pass out."

The idea of blacking out in front of him is enough to turn my stomach, especially with his chastising tone, but there's something to be said for the image of him gathering me up off the floor, gently patting my cheek and calling to me until I came to. He might roll his eyes while he's doing it—*silly Tzipporah*—but he wouldn't panic, and he wouldn't leave me facedown in the carpet. I'm sure of it.

He drinks with more control than I had and reaches for a strawberry. Elan likes strawberries. Something I should remember now that we'll be living together.

AT THE DOOR to his apartment—no, *our* apartment, I reach for the mezuzah and bring my fingers to my mouth. The one gracing the doorway to my old apartment had been wood, but this one is metal and glass. Regardless, I know if I were to crack the small, narrow boxes open, I'd find the same thing inside: verses from the Torah inscribed on parchment. Kissing the mezuzah is a habit I used to feel self-conscious about, but no more. Now I'd no more come or go without touching it than I'd leave without putting clothes on. Elan does the same, and then we're standing in a hallway.

We'd discussed staying in a hotel for our first night as a married couple as lots of people do, but with class tomorrow I'd said I'd feel more comfortable going straight home. Elan had seemed slightly disconcerted by yet another eccentricity of mine, but not inclined to argue.

I've been in this apartment a few times; a couple while Rivka was alive and once while the family was sitting shiva for her. I remember the doors that line the narrow passageway, the peculiar shade of green—a not-quite-avocado. I wonder if he'd be averse to me painting it? These are my thoughts as I walk through the hall of my new home, where I'll live from now on. With Elan. I follow his broad back to the living room and when we get there, he turns to me.

"Are you hungry?"

Seriously? We've just eaten enough to feed a small country. "No. Are you?"

He's a large man, but surely even he had his fill at the reception. We'd made a point of eating, both of us remembering how we'd been famished after our first weddings because we'd spent so much time visiting and taking pictures instead of enjoying the feast. Not this time.

"No, I just…" There's a quick shake of his head and that's when I realize that he's nervous. Elan, who I can't imagine being afraid of anything because he's so solid and dwarfs everything around him, is nervous. I make him uneasy.

"It's strange to have me in your home." The *your* to me is plural. I still think of this as Elan and Rivka's home. When his face darkens, I wonder if it's not because he thinks of it the same way. I can imagine them moving here as young newlyweds, can practically hear Rivka's vibrant laugh bouncing off the walls. He must have so many fond memories and here I am, awkward and so unlike her.

I won't ask to paint the hallway. I don't want him to feel as though I'm trying to erase her. He's allowed to still love her.

"Our home," he says, laying hands on my upper arms. His fingers reach nearly around my biceps and they're hot through the fabric of my wedding dress. The intimacy of the sensation makes me swallow.

"Of course." I try to smile, though I find it difficult to look in his eyes when I do. The touch reminds me that we'll be having more contact in the very near future. A lot more. And artless though I may be when it comes to men, I believe the expression on his face could be described as desire. Perhaps even lust?

Though it's probably a result of the epic dry spell he's endured, it makes me feel good. To know a man wants me. Not any man, but the man I've promised myself to, the man I've built fantasies around in the hopes that they'll sustain me.

His thumbs are stroking my arms and the purposeful contact curbs my breath. I haven't been touched for so long in a covetous way and I ache for it. *More.* When one of his hands leaves my body, I want to protest but it lands at the side of my neck before I can. It makes me sigh and take a step forward, closer to him. So close I can feel the heat of his body, hear the sound of his breath.

"Elan…"

"May I kiss you?"

"Of course." It's silly, but it delights me that he's asked. When his lips hit mine, I'm glad he gave me a warning. This is not a tentative meeting of unfamiliar mouths. This is hunger, pure and simple and it's echoed by the tightening of his hand at my neck. The squeeze of his fingers, knowing what they could take from me with all of their restrained power, floods me. Yes. It will be so easy to pretend with this man.

He tastes like wine and cake, the flavors of celebration lingering on his tongue as it tangles with mine and his beard scrapes against my face. It's at once exactly how I thought it would be and not at all. Scratchy but somehow soft, and outrageously masculine. Our bodies press together and I'm clutching the lapels of his suit like I might be blown away if I weren't. I can't help but notice he's hard for me.

We kiss hungrily until he separates us with a sharp inhale. "I want to do more than kiss you."

"I kind of hoped you would."

A deep, rumbling sound rises through him, something I'm tempted to call a growl, then he grasps my wrist and leads me back down the hallway, opening the third door and ushering me inside. The bed is large—I'm guessing two twins pushed together to make a king—and neatly made with the lace coverlet from my old bed already draped over it.

Then his hands are on me again and his mouth, oh his mouth. I reach up to thread my fingers through his hair and when I do, I find it soft and so dense I have to work my fingers into it. He makes an approving sound deep in his throat as I scratch gently at his scalp.

Soon our touches are wandering to arms, necks, shoulders and faces, abdomens and hips. There's a delicious frustration to it because we haven't pressed much farther than what everyone is allowed to see. I want more than that. I want my rights as his wife to his body, to that spot at the top of his head that's constantly covered by a kippah, but I'll get to see it soon enough.

He draws back, his dark eyes wild and his voice appealingly surly as he says, "Turn around."

When I do, he unbuttons my dress, his fingertips caressing the skin of my back. I wouldn't have thought the touch of a man so big could be so deft, but soon he's finished with the buttons and parts the fabric to reveal more skin.

I stand there, willing my breath steady though I'm going to start shaking. Or at least clutching my hands in my skirts. What is he looking at? I'm about to ask when he slips the satin over my shoulders and tugs the sleeves down my arms, the remainder of the dress following suit and puddling at my feet.

Then his hands are clenching around my biceps. While I'm sure he's *seen* the upper arms of women around the neighborhood, in his shop even, I doubt he's touched a woman in this intimate place since Rivka died. Has maybe not touched a woman at all, anywhere.

I hope I look beautiful to him, standing in my shoes, my underwear and my tichels. Bina had suggested wearing my hair down just for the day, but I couldn't, just couldn't. Not even under the veil. She'd offered the alternative of wearing a sheitel, which would be more typical of a bride here but it would have felt strange to me and I didn't need anything adding to my nerves. It's certainly not the first time I've bucked expectations, nor will it be the last.

Out of my clothes, I'm more conscious of my physique than I have been for a long time. I don't have a young woman's body any more, but I want to please him. He kneels behind me and removes my shoes before drawing my underwear over my hips and down my legs, issuing a grunted instruction of "step out."

And here I am. Naked in front of a man for the first time in five years. For the first time since my divorce. I hope with all my heart that this will be the last man who will see me this way. That I'll be able to give myself to him fully, perhaps even more than he knows. There's only one last piece of my plumage left to give way and though I see motion out of the corner of my eye, it takes longer for his touch to reach me than I'd expect, as if he hesitated.

But then his hands are roving the tightly wound scarves, searching for the place to start. He doesn't ask for help, so I don't give him any, but let him fumble until he finds the place where the ends are pinned. He unwinds the bound length and lets it rest against my back.

"I've been dreaming of this." His voice is thick with desire or emotion. It's difficult to tell which because I can't see his face. "Every night for weeks, I've dreamed of you coming to me. I could imagine your body, but this…this was a mystery."

Reverence. That's what colors the timbre of his voice.

I know what my students and the other faculty say about me and probably most of the strangers I see walking down the street. They think I'm foolish and old-fashioned and anti-feminist. I'm not. I understand that sometimes my secular and my religious beliefs come into conflict. I have no excuses to offer. It may seem hypocritical, and yet this is what feels right for me.

But I think if they could hear Elan's voice at this moment, his hoarse words, they might understand. Covering my hair isn't about being oppressed. It's about honoring my faith, but also about giving a gift and in so giving, bringing a man easily twice my weight and a good foot taller than I am to his knees. Having him so consumed with thoughts of me that I occupy his dreams.

With sweetly graceless movements, he begins to unwind the cloth from my hair and when he sees it, there's a whispered exclamation. "Red."

His movements become faster, greedy as he separates the scarves from my hair and the locks fall down my back. Then he's finger-combing through it, separating the strands that have been twisted together under my tichels all day. Five years is a long time to not get your hair cut and mine falls to my waist.

"No. Not red. Auburn," he says and I can't help but preen. I've always thought it was a pretty color and I'm glad he likes it.

We stumble awkwardly over to the bed—his side or mine?—and he pushes me onto it before he strips his own clothes. Perhaps someday he'll let me do it but for now I'm content to watch as he peels off his wedding finery and yes, his kippah.

I could stare at him all day, memorize the broad lines of him, but he doesn't give me the opportunity. He grasps my ankles and swings them onto the bed, making me collapse on the pillows in the process. My shocked giggle is cut off by him settling over me, his hips between my legs and an arm propping him up above me.

"What do you need from me, Tzipporah? Tell me. I won't have you until you're ready."

Bless those conscientious chossen teachers who make it clear to grooms that it's the man's responsibility to make sure his wife is ready and willing. People can talk smack about the keeping kosher and hair covering all they like, but this is definitely something Judaism got right.

I'm tempted to fantasize myself to wetness, keep my secrets tucked safe inside because he's already laid me bare enough for one day. But I don't want to take that from him, the opportunity to please his partner. Not after he's asked. And perhaps, if I'm the luckiest woman on earth, he might indulge me. And if he won't...

It'll be fine. It will. He's real enough, control distilled, that it'll be easy to tell stories about him in my mind while he lies atop me and thrusts inside. I'm lucky in some ways that orgasming is such a mental exercise for me. But what I wouldn't give to come from what was actually happening instead of the yarn I spin in my head...

So when he strokes his thumb across my cheek, his big hand cradling the side of my face, I tell him. "I..."

Well, I try.

"I..." Oh, big breath. Maybe if I hadn't studied him for so long from afar, I wouldn't notice the slight rise of the center of his eyebrows. But I have, so I do. This is his curious face. *What is my crazy wife going to say?*

"I like to be…hurt."

Even through my rapidly fluttering eyelashes I can see his eyes grow wide and his nostrils flare.

"Hurt?" he echoes, and the heat in my cheeks grows more intense.

"Yes." This is profoundly uncomfortable. Perhaps I should've kept this to myself after all. I can't take it back now, but maybe I can slowly back away from the elephant I've just lobbed into the middle of the room. "But—"

I don't need it. Yes, I do. This was part of the reason I left Brooks. Because he wouldn't give this to me. Couldn't. Why am I pretending that's not true?

"Do you like to be spanked, little bird?"

Now it's my turn to be surprised. His tone isn't cruel or mocking. It's sweetly enticing, like honey dripping from apples. Or perhaps something not quite as sweet. Darker, earthier, more lingering than honey. Molasses.

Breathing around the wings beating at my heart, I moisten my lips between my teeth.

"Yes."

"With just a hand or more than that?"

Thinking of what damage his substantial palms and strong fingers might do, I breathe, "A hand to start."

He nods. "To start."

"Yes."

"But perhaps something more than that?"

"Perhaps."

Turns out I don't actually need to be hurt to get turned on. All I need to do is talk about it with his dark eyes laser-focused on me. Between my legs, there's a growing heat and sensitivity. If he slipped a hand between us, he'd find me wet. But instead of reaching down to the apex of my thighs, he slides his hand toward the back of my neck, fingers twining in my hair and closing. It makes my lips part.

"And besides being hurt, are there other things?"

"Other things?" I try to look innocent, but the tightening at my scalp and the shake of his head tell me he's not buying it.

"Don't tease me. Tell me the truth. What else?"

The beat of wings about my lungs grows more intense and I struggle to breathe. "Restraint. I like to be restrained."

"My little bird likes to be kept in a cage?"

"That's not how it feels." It's difficult to explain, but even though I'm being controlled, even when—maybe especially when—I can't move an inch, it makes me feel like I can fly away. Like the strings that keep me tethered to the ground have been cut and I can finally launch myself into the sky where I belong.

"It's not, is it?" His fingers knead the nape of my neck as he studies me. "It makes you feel free."

Perhaps my brain has been too crowded with anxiety or sensual thoughts, but this is the first time it occurs to me that Elan is neither shocked nor appalled by my requests and seems—dare I hope?—*conversant* in these matters? But before I can ask, he presses on.

"And how do you like to be set free? Rope? Leather? Chains?"

I get the urge to rub my wrists because I can practically feel the fetters as he talks. But that would be rude and besides, I wouldn't be able to reach my hands around his broad back to touch. "Anything that won't leave a mark the next morning?"

I curse myself for the desperate hope in my voice. I'd had to don long sleeves for days when Brooks left evidence of our play after I'd asked him not to. I should've known better about the handcuffs, but I let him. I didn't want to tell him no after he'd actually agreed to try. Not smart.

"Anywhere? Or just where your clothes won't cover?"

"Just where my clothes won't cover."

"Fair. There's plenty of you left to work with." If the eyes are the windows to the soul, I can see him turning this over and over behind his dark irises. Which brings me back to my thought.

"Have you done…this before?"

If the lighting weren't low and his beard didn't cover so much of his face, I might say he blushes. "I don't particularly want to discuss it but the short answer is yes."

"How did you know about it? And it's kosher?" I hadn't wanted to ask in fear that I'd be told it's not allowed. Besides, my face probably would've caught on fire if I'd asked my kallah teacher or Rabbi Horowitz.

Elan smiles, a small laugh vibrating his chest against

mine, the thick mat of hair scraping against my soft and sensitive skin. The rough contact makes my nipples harden against him and I wonder if he notices. "I had an excellent and very thorough chossen teacher and Rabbi Horowitz happens to be quite…liberal in these matters. He's adamant about pleasing wives. Why do you think Bina's so cheerful all the time?"

I break into a nervous giggle. Surely talking about the rabbi's sex life is some kind of no-no.

"Enough talking for now, though. I think you might be ready for me and if not, I have some ideas."

He rolls to the side and I immediately miss the weight of him spreading my thighs. I start to close them but he grasps above my knee and tsks. "Stay open for me."

A whimper escapes my throat. What am I, some kind of animal? When he slides his palm along the inside of my thigh, I don't care. If he wants me to be an animal, an animal I'll be. He stops just short of where I'm throbbing for him, barely brushing the nest of curls, and then coasts his hand over my stomach and ribcage up to my breast.

"Hands above your head."

Oh. I obey, resting them on the pillow. His gaze travels over me, stopping at certain points along the way, all the lush, forbidden places.

"Do you trust me to tie you?"

The truth is that it was far more frightening to confess that I want to be tied than the actual prospect of being tied is. "Yes."

I expect him to stand, perhaps rummage under the bed, but he doesn't. Instead he squeezes the breast he's been palming. Softly at first and then increasingly hard until his fingers are digging into the sensitive flesh and I make a noise.

It's funny, the things you know only about the people you've been intimate with. The sounds they make, how their faces look as they come. More small pieces of myself that I'll surrender to him. *Take them, please. Just promise to handle them with care.*

He continues to work at me, not heeding the sound and I'm glad. It's beginning to hurt but in a way I like. In a way that, strangely, feels good. Then he grasps my nipple and pinches, the pressure sending a sizzle of pleasure straight between my legs where I'm exposed. The pressure is deliciously hard and he doesn't let up. Just holds the sensitive peak between his fingers. The steady even pressure is a turn on as he stares at his hold on me. "Someday I'll use clamps on you. Leave my hands free. But first I want to train you to my touch."

Another ungainly squeak is forced through my throat because the idea is shockingly but undeniably arousing. Again he ignores it and then squeezes harder. Hard enough to make me squeal, hard enough that my back arches. Only when his free hand grips my wrists and forces them down do I realize my hands came off the bed. "Stay still. You're mine to do with as I please and I want you to keep your hands above your head. And don't close your legs. Open for me. Always open for me."

His scolding makes me shamefully hot for him. Whenever Brooks deigned to do this, I always felt like he was pretending. Like it was a foolish game he didn't really want to play. With Elan, it feels real and the authenticity fans the flames of my desire. It's better than I'd imagined.

He toys with me for a while, leisurely in his actions like he has all the time in the world to make me squirm underneath him. And I suppose he does. Where else am I going to go?

He switches to the other breast and continues to torture and tease me until I'm tossing my head on the pillow. I only realize I'm sweating when he stops his torment and wipes away some strands of hair that have become matted to my face.

"Aren't you a fun little plaything?" His gently mocking words make me even hotter for him and doubly so when he demands, "Answer me."

"Yes."

"Yes, what?"

My breath has gone short and if he didn't have my hands pinned above my head I'd pinch myself. Is he—

"Yes, sir?"

"I think a stronger word is called for. Out there, we live as man and wife, as equals. In here, though…this is a different matter. We'll have our own little contract that says you've signed yourself over to me and my wishes. You're going to call me master."

The bird inside me that usually flutters around, beating at my ribs and crowding my heart, sometimes hiding behind my lungs like a shy partridge—suddenly spreads its wings and the tips of the feathers catch on fire. And when I whisper, "Yes, master," it bursts fully into flame, rising out of my chest like a phoenix.

"There you go," he says, stroking my hair. "That wasn't so bad now, was it?"

"No, master."

The academic in me wants to slow down, take a step back, examine this from every angle. But the submissive part of me rejoiced in saying the word and I want to do it again and again. There will be plenty of time to think later.

"Good girl. You're a quick learner, are you?" I flush, because only sometimes, as he well knows. But in this, I desperately want to please and it comes so much easier to me. Particularly with his guidance.

"Yes, master."

"Yes. That's how you should answer me whenever I ask a question. Do you understand?"

"Yes, master."

He nods his satisfaction and then releases me, making me miss his touch immediately. Crouching naked by the bed, he delves underneath. The sound of something dragging across the hardwood floor reaches my ears. When he comes to his feet, it's with several hanks of rope and I'm surprised by the muted, deep purple. It's beautiful. And not something you have just for the hell of it.

I'd also be willing to wager those aren't the only ones he has. My mind starts to dream up a rainbow of rope kept just out of my sight, but I'm called back by the soft fall of the carefully tied bundles on the bed beside me. He takes one up and unravels it, the long strands falling to the ground. I've seen pictures of the results of this kind of play, but never the process in person. I'm fascinated.

With the same skill and concentration I've long admired him for in his shop, he handles the rope, and moves to the foot of the bed where he grasps my ankle. "Injuries? Anything else I should know?"

"No injuries. I just…I need to be able to breathe."

He sets to work without acknowledging my answer, wrapping and tying the line around my ankle, making a thick cuff out of strand upon strand, the cord winding higher and higher until it's just below the curve of my calf muscle. Then he uses the ends to attach me to the bedframe and proceeds almost without pause to the other side, creating a mirror image and leaving my legs bent. It's quickly made apparent why as he fashions more wide cuffs just above my knees and, tugs just roughly enough to make me gasp, spreads my legs wider before tying off under the mattress.

He bends over me with yet another hank of rope and sets to work on my wrists. The bonds are tight but not uncomfortable and I feel…held. Even when he's not touching me.

"You look very pretty in rope, little bird. In the future I'll take more time with you, but for now…" His eyes rake down my spread out and bound body. I've always thought of him as a bear, but perhaps wolf is more apt. "For now I want to be inside you. Inside my wife."

He climbs deftly onto the bed, settling between my thighs on his knees. He's so erect it looks almost painful. During one of our awkward courtship conversations, we'd had a perfunctory discussion of contraception. Yes, we both wanted children, probably sooner rather than later because I'm thirty-seven. No, neither of us had diseases. In that at least I'd been lucky. Brooks may have strayed from our marriage bed, but at least he didn't bring anything back.

It's the first time I've had sex with the intent of pro-creation. Or at least, without effort to prevent pregnancy. It feels more intimate somehow, knowing we could make a life, even though we're essentially strangers.

He grips my thighs, fingers digging into me in a way that's likely to leave bruises. If the rope and the tone weren't enough to make me feel conquered, this touch would do it. I strain against the ropes, trying to make myself more vulnerable to him, as if he needs the help.

Soon, he's leaning over me, propping himself up on a hand by my shoulder and finally, finally, he puts a hand between my legs, parting me gently and making an aggressively appreciative noise. "This is what you wanted. This is what you need. Isn't it?"

"Yes, master."

With my acquiescence, he pushes a finger inside, making it two when there's no resistance. The rhythmic thrusts feel incredible and make me want more of him, all of him. Make me crave the heavy thickness resting hot on my thigh.

He doesn't fuck me for long this way and I'm glad. Instead he drags his fingers from my body and plants his hand on the bed, containing me. Then he's easing into me, the stretch making me aware of exactly how full I'll be when he's completely seated. Breached. Conquered. Possessed. That's exactly how it feels when he's in me to the hilt. And it gets better when he starts to move.

Moving slowly, he rocks his hips that are spreading my thighs even wider than the rope. When he seems confident he's not going to hurt me, not really, he thrusts harder and the force is delicious.

I tilt my hips up to meet him, take him deeper inside. He takes it as an invitation and the thrusting changes to outright pounding. It doesn't take long for me to be close and I realize he hasn't told me… Am I supposed to ask? But perhaps he can tell, by some quickening of my breath, some change in the pitch of my encouraging moans, I'm nearly there.

"Fly for me, little bird."

His low command trips something inside of me and I plummet down, my body seizing before rising up into an incredible climax. *Fly for me*, he said. And I am. The flight made more rewarding by his desire for it, his permission. I cry out, saying his name, as I pull at my bonds. He lets me ride out my orgasm, rocking up against him in an uneven rhythm to catch the last of it, scrambling for the aftershocks as if I'll never come again.

When I'm limp and replete beneath him, he kisses me: my cheekbone, just above my eyebrow, my lips. I kiss him back, a languid press of my lips, a dreamy sweep of my tongue. But a stirring inside me reminds me I'm the only one who's satisfied.

"Do you have anything to say to me?"

"Thank you, master?"

"Quick study indeed."

His praise—or perhaps it's my orgasm—makes me glow and I smile at him.

"Is there anything else you want from me?"

"I want you to come. I want you to use me, finish inside of me. Let me know I please you."

"You do, Tzipporah, you do." With that confirmation, he's moving again, fucking me harder and faster than before. I wouldn't be able to get off from this, but I sure do enjoy it. Especially knowing that he's taking what he wants from me, not caring for my pleasure because I've been sated. With a last hard thrust that makes me yelp because he's reached someplace so deep inside, he comes, his groan of satisfaction drowning out my desultory protest. The sharp pain is already fading into an ache and the next presses of him inside of me are less forceful.

If I weren't tied down, I'd take his head in my hands, thread my fingers through his hair. As it is, I press my face to the side of his neck and listen to his slowing breath. At last he pushes up on his elbows and reaches over my head. The rope around my hands loosens and then unfurls. Still inside me, he rubs one wrist and then the other. When he rolls off, he offers me a cloth and I press it between my restrained legs. He uses a second to clean off and then stretches alongside me.

I rest my hands on my stomach and notice the rope has pressed into my skin, imprinting a pattern in red.

"It will fade by tomorrow." He sounds apologetic and he should do anything but apologize.

"I wasn't concerned. I was…admiring them."

"You should." He reaches over and traces line upon line, evidence of his possession. "You mark nicely."

Oh. On the extremely rare occasions I'd gotten Brooks to play hard enough to leave bruises and welts, I'd look at them whenever I'd get the chance. I didn't tell him because I didn't think he'd understand. He walked in on me once while I was getting ready for a shower. I'd been holding out a large hand mirror at arm's length, reflecting my reflection so I could marvel at the evidence of our play he'd left on my back. I'd never seen him look so confused or disgusted. That might have been when he realized we were irrevocably different.

The caress of Elan's fingers against the impressed design on my wrists is gentle. Tender even. We lie there in silence until he speaks.

"Was all of that okay? You didn't tell me to stop. You know you can always tell me to stop and I will."

He hadn't said it before, but I hadn't been worried. It was stupid of me but I'd been so thrilled I hadn't stopped to insist and I did trust him to stop if I asked him to. Completely reckless. I'm glad he's correcting the mistake by talking about it, no matter how uncomfortable it may be.

"I…I liked everything."

"Good. Is there anything you absolutely don't want me to do?"

I give an awkward shrug. "I'll try anything once. As long as you promise to be careful. And I don't want any permanent marks."

"That's reasonable. But if there's ever something you didn't like… Well, I won't promise not to do it again, but it's good information to have."

I murmur my thanks and assure him again, "So far, so good. But, my legs…"

It's not uncomfortable, but it's been a while that I've been immobilized and I'd like to move. He glances down and then turns back to me. "Are they numb?"

"No, master."

He makes a noncommittal noise and goes back to tracing the marks on my wrists. I should be indignant, but somehow his oblique refusal lets me relax. I don't have to choose even in this. After a while, he pets my hair and I soften further. So much so that I drift off, tied to my marital bed.

CHAPTER THREE

F I HAD thought better of it, I wouldn't have had an October wedding. Although a month-long engagement was already raising a few eyebrows and shorter would've raised more and higher because that's short even by frum standards, the confusion at the university may be worse. When I tell my Wednesday morning students they should call me Professor Klein, they look at me blankly. Particularly since I saw them on Monday, when I was Professor Berger.

One backwards-ball-capped boy who sits in the back of the lecture hall who I think spends far more time checking Mets standings on his cell than paying attention to my class raises his hand.

"Yes, Scott?"

I make a point of memorizing my students' names early in the semester. I've found it makes them care more to know that I realize when Scott or Lauren hasn't handed in their homework than ID number 6009921. I hope it also makes it easier for them to come talk to me if they're struggling since they already know I think of them as people.

He looks surprised, though, as they so often do, because most of my colleagues don't bother. "Why?"

My face gets warm but I hope it doesn't translate to a blush because I'm not embarrassed. I just don't want to spend half the class answering questions about Orthodox wedding conventions. That class isn't until November.

I hold up my left hand, thankful for the thick band on my finger. Something everyone understands. "I got married on Tuesday. And as a wedding present from you all, I'd like to move on with class. We've got a lot of material to cover this semester and I can guarantee my personal life isn't going to be on your final exam."

A few congratulations and a smattering of applause sound in the small auditorium and I wave and say thank you but flip open to my notes and start in on my introduction to religious texts. "How many of you have ever read the Bible?"

WEDNESDAYS I COME home from work on the earlier side, around four. After the divorce but before I married Elan, I would stay in my office or at the library until late. It was better to be where there was at least the opportunity for human interaction than to go home to my empty apartment.

Over time, a couple of those late nights turned into Torah study at the shul and a weekly game of mahjong at

Bina's house. It's one of the things I like best about this life I've chosen: when they say community, they mean it. For better or for ill, of course—what with the politics and petty grievances—but I've found it mostly for the better. You never have to be alone.

I let myself into the apartment I think of as Elan's and put my things away. Maybe someday I'll feel as if this place is ours, but it's only been a single day. I spend some time unpacking boxes in the unused bedroom I've taken for my office before it's time to make dinner.

On the meat shelf in the refrigerator, there's a neatly wrapped package he must have brought home during his lunch break or perhaps on his way to afternoon prayer services. It has a note on it, "For Dinner" spelled out in his methodical, blocky print. When I was trying to keep kosher as a single person, I'd mostly kept a vegetarian diet. It feels positively indulgent to have meat for dinner more than one night a week, never mind two nights in a row. I suppose that's one of the benefits of being the butcher's wife.

There's enough chicken in the package to feed half a dozen people. I'm about to wrap half of it back up to put in the freezer but I realize I'm doing my meal calculus based off how much *I* eat. One serving for me and five for Elan is probably about right.

I turn on some music and set to work, pounding and breading the chicken, setting some mushrooms to sauté on the stove, boiling water for the noodles. Food has been one of the hardest things for me to acclimate to. Not just keeping strict kosher, although I'm still kind of a disaster at that—the number of times I've had to ask Rabbi Horowitz's opinion on how to kasher a specific kitchen implement is downright embarrassing. I bet he and Bina keep one of those little wipeboards usually found on industrial sites: *It Has Been X Days Since Tzipporah's Screwed Up Keeping Kosher.* There are also the cravings for foods I used to have. Bacon cheeseburgers. Lobster rolls. Veal Parmesan.

Chicken piccata is one of the things I've been able to modify. Though I miss the buttery sauce I used to prepare, the recipe I make now with wine and broth is a decent substitute and it's worth eating the kosher version. The same cannot be said for kosher pizza. That might be the saddest food in the universe.

My timing is perfect. Elan arrives just as I'm taking the asparagus from the oven.

"Smells good." How is it that he makes a compliment sound like an allegation?

I tame my grimace into a mere purse of my lips. "No butter. I promise."

He grunts and I roll my eyes. Not that it's completely unreasonable of him to be suspicious, but I wish he'd trust me more than that. Although I suppose when one of his first experiences with me was me having a complete and utter meltdown because I messed up my brisket and I had to admit during our courtship that it's something I continue to bungle regularly, it's not surprising that's his default. Hopefully over time, dutifully prepared meals, or at least realizing I'll always tell him if I've made a mistake, will sand the sharp edges of his low expectations away, because I can't live under this kind of scrutiny forever.

"What is this…music?"

Right. Given how conservative his family is, Elan probably listened to mostly, if not exclusively, Jewish music growing up. Does he still? If so, I don't think Regina Spektor counts.

"It's the clean version," I mutter after telling him the artist and the album, self-consciousness drawing my shoulder blades tight together. I've never been much for movies and TV so giving those up hasn't been a problem, but there's no way I'm letting go of my enormous iTunes library. Although if he adheres to the prohibition against men listening to women sing, I should be respectful of that. "But I could change it if you want. To a man."

"It's fine," he says, his brows drawing together as if he's trying to acclimate himself to the idea that he's going to be listening to pop music for the rest of his life. If he is, it doesn't take long. The muscles in his forehead release and there's a small shrug. Good, because I think Pink is up next in my library.

After we've sat down to eat and said the blessing, he pokes at the chicken as if I might have poisoned it.

"It's kosher, I swear. No butter, no cream, no cheese. I didn't even touch the dairy shelf. I used the meat utensils and dishes for everything. I checked all the labels. There was no blood in the eggs." Tears start to sting behind my eyes as I recite my list. To think I used to enjoy cooking. I'm sure when, or at this point *if*, I'm more proficient, I'll enjoy it again. But for now, it reduces me to a bundle of nerves and he's not helping matters any. I'm going to develop a phobia.

I knew this would be an adjustment and I thought I had prepared for it, but I wasn't ready for this. Feeling like I'm under a microscope, having all my secular holdovers examined and poked at. What is he going to say when he sees all of my books left over from my university degrees and the modern art prints I have on the walls of my office? Maybe nothing because I'm certainly not the only frum person to have non-Jewish books or art in their home, but I don't know.

My hands have closed into fists on either side of my plate and I can't meet his eyes. I probably shouldn't have snapped at him, but it would be nice if there were at least one place on earth where I felt comfortable, where I didn't feel judged for being too Jewish or not Jewish enough. It would be even better if that place were my home.

His hand comes to rest over mine on the table and he shushes me. "I apologize, Tzipporah. I'll try to be more...optimistic."

An image of Elan frolicking in a field with a crown of daisies on his head nearly makes me laugh. I don't need him to be some Pollyanna, but a little bit of faith from the man I married wouldn't hurt.

"I appreciate that. Thank you."

Despite our détente, we eat with a bare minimum of conversation, my head occupied with all the things I'll have to do tomorrow: unpacking the rest of my things, office hours, a late seminar. When dinner's over, Elan helps me clear and clean up the kitchen. Though some of the frum men I know act as though cooking is the women's domain, nearly all of them help with the aftermath of a meal. And if he hadn't cooked before, I suppose Elan lost that luxury while Rivka was ill. He told me himself he's capable of putting together a meal.

After scrubbing the pans, I dry off my hands on the dishtowel and turn to go to bed. I'm exhausted. Elan blocks my path though, his broad shoulders taking up nearly the entire passageway. It's a wonder he doesn't have to turn sideways to move about these older apartments with their narrow hallways, or duck through the low doorframes.

"I thought…" He clears his throat, awkwardness personified. "If you weren't too tired… We might…"

Is he propositioning me? Part of me wants to decline. I'm tired from my long day of classes, from the pressure cooker the kitchen's become for me, from his wariness. But another part of me stirs. Perhaps sex wouldn't be a bad idea. An orgasm is a pretty good cure for emotional turmoil and despite discomfiture in other areas, I think we please each other in this one. And it's good to establish these habits early on, right? Begin as you mean to go on? I have no intention of returning to a sexless marriage.

"Um, sure."

He holds his hands out to his sides. "We don't have to. If you don't—"

"No. I think that's a good idea." And I appreciate

him offering. Excellent chossen teacher indeed, teaching his students to make overtures.

Some of the tension leaves Elan's shoulders. "Come, then."

I'm only too glad to follow him down the hallway and into the bedroom. Once the door is closed, he turns on me and any awkwardness is gone. He looks powerful and virile and I have the urge to get on my knees for him. Perhaps someday he'll command me to.

For now, he steers me to the center of the room and removes my clothes, running hands over the parts of me only he gets to see: my upper arms, my collarbones, from my knees to my hips. All the places so much of the world has decided have become public property. But for us, they're private treasures. When he picks at my tichels, I'm glad I never went back to having my hair flow free even after the divorce.

While I was taking classes at the outreach center and attending seminary, it had elicited some whispers. Here, divorcees and widows tend to stop covering their heads, in part to signify their single status. I had already stood out because most of the women here who cover do so with sheitels instead of tichels. I'd assumed that's what people had found odd—my colorful scarves instead of a wig—but apparently not. Bina had finally pulled me aside. "You know you don't have to keep your head covered. Not until you're married. It's not like it earns you extra credit."

My face had burned. I hadn't realized that's what people thought of me—that I was trying to out-frum the frum. I hadn't been. But... "I started covering when I was married. And once I started, to go back seemed..."

Horrifying. It would've been like walking around naked and I couldn't bear it. My hair had become something to be kept private, for only my husband—and hopefully the man who would be willing to dominate me—and the thought of going back made my stomach clench. I suppose I could've switched to a sheitel to make it less obvious but tying my scarves on had become as much a part of my morning routine as brushing my teeth.

Bina's kind face had lit with understanding. My discomfort must have been glaringly obvious. "Ah. I understand. Don't worry. You might deter some suitors, that's all."

Let them be deterred. If that had been all it took, I hadn't been interested anyhow. I had wanted someone who could handle me, in all senses of the word. It seems my stubbornness may have paid off.

Once my hair is free, drifting down to my waist, Elan steps away and looks at me, his gaze intent. It doesn't shame me though, doesn't make me want to cover myself. It makes me feel proud and alluring.

He sits on the edge of the bed, his feet touching the floor. I wait for instructions, wondering if he means to admire me until I squirm and plead with him. I'd do it too. His attention alone is starting to turn me on.

"Come here."

His voice is softly commanding and it arouses me more than if it had been a harsh order. He has so much confidence, so much control, he doesn't need to raise his voice or be cruel to get what he wants.

I approach him slowly, not breaking eye contact, and he pats one of his thick thighs. "Over my knee, little bird."

Oh. Everything about this—him clothed, me nude; his self-possessed directives; and now the invitation to be spanked—it flips switches of desire inside me, sending me into overdrive, leaving some of my stress behind. *Yes, please.*

I climb onto the bed and drape myself over his lap, his legs sturdy and warm underneath my torso. He adjusts me slightly, urging me to arch my back to offer myself to him more fully, and telling me to turn my head because I'm going to be there for a while.

Pillowing my head on folded arms, I enjoy him stroking my back and my behind. It also serves to remind me exactly how big and heavy his hand is. And that's going to be what's making firm and repeated contact with my butt in the not-so-distant future. The anticipation is delectable and I would bet money that my eyes have gone glassy already.

More so when his other hand winds into my hair and pins me down to the bed, keeping tension on my scalp. Not enough to hurt, but enough to make me feel controlled, tamed. Perfect. That's when the first strike lands.

Hard but not too hard, his palm lands against me and I moan. I love it for everything it is but also for what it's not. The motion's not apologetic or half-hearted. He wants to hit me and I want to be hit. I wiggle my hips and I can hear the smile in his voice when he says, "You like that."

It sounds more like an observation than a question, but just in case, I answer. "Yes, master."

"Good."

Then he's spanking me in earnest, one blow quickly following the other. He smacks me all over, turning me red from my hips to the tops of my thighs. When my whole bottom is heated, he focuses on one spot, striking me over and over. The force is harder and harder and I didn't know a hand-spanking could hurt so badly. Soon my attention is zeroed in to the same spot his has been. I can't think of anything except how much the next hit is going to sting.

Just when I think I can't take it anymore, he diffuses his attention, spreading the slaps all over. If my color had faded, it's back now, probably more vivid than before. When he's set me on fire, he returns to that same wicked spot. I whimper a protest and he clucks at me.

"Is this not fun? Is this not what you had in mind?"

It is and I can feel the wetness gathering between my legs to prove it, but it's complicated. My enjoyment isn't unqualified and if the mocking in his tone is any indication, he knows it.

"It is, master."

"You're going to take a dozen more then."

That doesn't sound so bad. Altogether he must've hit me a hundred times. A dozen is paltry. At least I think so until his palm lands next and I squeal. It's the hardest he's hit me yet and it's in that devilish place. Then there's another. And another. I'm going to have an outline of his hand on my ass for a week.

He pauses when he's halfway through, rubbing at me. Even the gentle touch makes me feel sore and abused. "Halfway done. Are you going to relax for me, little bird? Let yourself go?"

Is that what he's been waiting for? Is that what he wants? For me to fall apart? I want to, have been choking back tears and cries, partly because I want to be strong for him, prove that I can take everything he can possibly dish out. It's not all stubborn pride, though. There's a component of fear. If I let on exactly how much he's hurting me, will he stop?

That's what would happen with Brooks. Just when I was enjoying it the most, just when I would think he could push me higher, he'd get uncomfortable with my reactions, my noises, and he'd stop. Leave me stranded all alone, deserted in this incredibly uncomfortable purgatory of being inches from relief and not being able to get it.

Perhaps Elan senses my overwrought hesitation because he pinches me on the fuzzy border of where I'm now certain there'll be a bruise. "How about this? How about I just spank you 'til you cry?"

A dream come true. "Please, master."

He starts in on me again and this time I don't try to protect myself. I just let it come. All the pain, all the sounds, all the tension of my life lately, everything pours out of me and the tears follow close behind. When I've broken down, he turns me over and cradles me in his lap, pulling my head to his shoulder and stroking my hair.

"That's better, isn't it?"

"Y-yes, m-m-master." I cling to him while I sob and he pets me.

After a few minutes, he urges me to spread my legs and I hide my face against his chest because I know how wet he's going to find me. It's embarrassing. Or at least I think it will be, but the approving noise he makes when his fingers come in contact with my very core makes me flush with pleasure.

He strokes me between my legs, makes leisurely circles around my clit before pressing inside of me. "You're so ready. But I wonder…what do you taste like?"

Continuing to toy with me, making me squirm against him and the very obvious erection pressed between my hip and his belly, he goes on. "Are you sweet? Earthy? I'd bet anything there's a little tang to you. I'm going to find out."

He shifts me onto the bed, the soft sheets rough against my tender behind as he scoots me back and forces my thighs apart, spreading me out with his thumbs before dipping his head and, oh, yes, tasting me.

That's what it feels like at first, too. Like he's sampling, analyzing. Trying to figure out exactly what my flavor is, the exact composition of my palate.

"I was right," he announces, looking up at me from between my legs. "A definite tang."

I laugh and cover my face because I just can't help it.

All of my emotions have been brought to the surface and any scratch will let them through.

"Don't cover your face. I want to watch you."

I've got no energy to protest so instead I lie back, close my eyes and let my hands drift into my hair. I feel like a goddess as he worships me, testing with his tongue and lips and teeth exactly what kind of combination of licks, kisses and bites make me squirm. He's surprisingly precise in his movements; even in this he exhibits control. It's so good I might die.

He's had me riding the edge for minutes when he takes my clit into his mouth and sucks before biting. My whole body shudders because it's exquisite and an equally trembling sound is forced from my throat.

"That's right," he murmurs while his beard scrapes against the sensitive skin of my inner thigh. "Spread your wings, little bird. I'm going to make you fly."

And he does, driving me back to the edge before shoving me over. He's holding me down as well as he can but I wish he'd tied me because it doesn't feel safe out here. It feels like I might fall to the earth from a great height.

But just when I open my eyes and start to sit up in a panic, he climbs over me, trapping me against the mattress, his hips pressing between my legs, his desire glaringly obvious as he rocks against me.

"I'll give you a minute, but I have to have you."

"I don't need a minute. But I'd like to…" I reach between us, palming his length through his pants and giving him a gentle squeeze. "…return the favor."

He closes his eyes and groans. "No."

"But…" Surely with all the liberal ideas he has about sex he can't hold to a strict interpretation on the prohibition of spilling of seed? I've been told oral and even anal were okay if it wasn't to the exclusion of having sex in a way that could get you pregnant. So what's his problem?

"No." His eyes snap open and I don't dare argue though I feel a bit chastised. "I didn't mean to sound harsh. It's just when I was growing up, that particular rule was practically beaten into us and it's stuck with me. I have a hard time."

"You don't have to come in my mouth."

He makes a strangled sound and then shakes his head, the corner of his mouth curling up. "That's the thing, Tzipporah. At this very second? I can't be sure I have that kind of self-control."

A meek "okay" is all I can muster because I'm floored by his confession. I make him that crazy. Granted, if what he's said is true, he probably didn't do much, if any, masturbating in the past few years and was perhaps so deprived he started finding melons and baked goods tempting in an inappropriate way. Who cares? It still makes me happy.

It doesn't take him long to strip his clothes and then he's pressing inside of me. I take him, all of him, laying my hands on his shoulder blades and holding onto him as he rocks his hips. Soon, he's thrusting into me, making the fire on my butt come alive again as he drives me into the mattress over and over again. As if I couldn't tell, his teeth sinking viciously into my shoulder tell me he's there. He shudders against me, releasing a groan that reverberates through his ribcage as he pulses inside me. Perhaps this is how we'll find our way to each other.

CHAPTER FOUR

E LAN HAS VOLUNTEERED to cook on Thursdays when I teach an evening class. It's very generous of him. He even rescheduled his weekly learning with his brother Moyshe to a different night, and though he didn't say so I know he'll leave the shop early to do it too. Not that his nephew and Reuven aren't perfectly capable of minding Klein Brothers for a couple of hours, but Elan likes to be there.

Emerging from the hot oven of the subway station with a flock of other frum around me, my shoulders drop. Home. I'm back in a neighborhood where more people look like me than don't, and the ones who don't are accustomed to Orthodox, many even stricter than I am. I love my job and while I'm teaching, it's easy to forget that my students and colleagues think I'm odd. They've become acclimated to the way I dress and I've gotten pretty good at speaking two different Englishes depending on where I am, but when the lecture stops and I have to walk through campus where people stare as I pass, it's impossible to ignore. I can't wait for colder weather when it won't be quite so obvious.

Once inside the apartment building, the sounds particular to each family—already familiar to me after just over a week—fill the halls as I climb the stairs. Mr. and Mrs. Friedman shouting at each other because they're both nearly deaf, the Cohens' eight children making the kind of ruckus only a herd of young ones can make, and the strains of violin music leaking from under the Rosenthals' door. I'm not sure how someone who can't play on Friday evenings or Saturdays makes a living as a musician but apparently it can be done.

When I open the door to our apartment, I'm hit by an olfactory wave. Curry.

Elan had asked me on one of our dates about the foods I missed since starting to keep kosher. Curry was on the list. Lamb, beef, chicken, I don't care. I never made it myself but it had been one of my go-to takeout options. No longer because though we have Middle Eastern food, an excellent Chinese restaurant, and there are rumors a sushi counter will be opening its doors, Indian cuisine hasn't quite made its way to Forest Park. But here it is, the unmistakable smell of curry wafting into the hallway.

I divest myself of my things and head to the kitchen where Elan is standing over a couple of pots on the meat side of the stove.

"I'm home, Elan." He probably heard my shuffling and dropping things in the hallway, but just in case I wanted to announce myself. I don't need to startle him over hot burners.

"Mmm." His distracted grunt doesn't bother me. Indeed, when I see his face, it's in a rictus of concentration so fierce I'd be surprised if he noticed if he set himself on fire.

"You made curry?"

"I have *tried* to make curry," he corrects me.

I smother the laugh rising because last week's attempt at lamb chops did not go well. He puts down the spoon he's been using to stir and reaches into his pocket, pulling out his wallet and holding it between us.

"Would you mind putting this in the bedroom? I meant to put it away earlier, but I forgot."

I carry it to the bedroom, knowing precisely where on his dresser it belongs. He's quite orderly and I try to keep my things the same way, lest he develop another complaint about me. My natural state is somewhat more…cluttered. But just as I'm about to return the worn leather billfold to its place, I stop in my tracks. There are several things laid out on my side of the bed.

A large metal ring, several bundles of rope of different colors and thicknesses, a hairbrush, three canes, and a pile of clamps of various sizes. Oh, my.

And oh, that wily man. I don't believe for a minute that he "forgot" his wallet in his pocket. He meant for me to see these things. He meant to make me ruminate on them, think about what he's going to do with them. Maybe to distract me from the quality—or lack thereof—of the curry?

Two can play at this game, Elan. You think you have a

flighty, scatterbrained wife? I can do that.

I stroll back, casual as can be, to where he's scooping out some curry onto beds of rice. It really does smell delicious and it looks like curry too. He hands me a plate and raises an eyebrow.

"Hungry?"

Is my husband flirting with me? I can play that game too.

"Very." The exaggerated syllables draw his attention and Elan's eyes are riveted to my lips.

"See anything you like?"

I want to wipe the cocky look right off his handsome face. Instead, I narrow my eyes and tip my head. "Everything looks very…enticing."

He shakes his head, the corner of his mouth curling up into an almost piratical smile. I suddenly want to be pillaged. Quite badly. But first things first.

We sit down at the table, say our prayers and start to eat. The curry—beef with onions, peppers, broccoli and cashews—is delicious and I don't think it's just because I'm famished from my long day.

"Thank you for making dinner, Elan. It's very good. And curry." I smile so he knows I appreciate it, how he remembered and went out of his way.

He spears a piece of meat on his fork. "Yes, well, I had to make something."

A few of the bubbles in my champagne euphoria pop. Could he not just do something nice for me and admit he was being nice? He tends to be considerate of me but there's a distinct lack of affection. I try to tell myself fondness is something that grows over time and we've only planted the seeds. It's ridiculous to expect that some great riot of warmth would've sprung from the earth overnight.

We make very small talk over the rest of our meal. Not that he's usually some chatty Cathy, but he's particularly reticent this evening, even my most carefully crafted questions barely eliciting one-word responses. In part because we're both devouring our food, but also because we're eager to get on to the evening's other activities.

A metal ring, rope, a hairbrush, canes, and clamps. It's enough to make me shift in my seat just thinking about it.

After we've hastily cleared and cleaned up the kitchen, he gestures down the hall with his arm. "After you."

It's possible I let my hips sway more than usual as I walk the short distance, wondering if he notices the extra swish in the skirts around my calves. Or perhaps he's focused on my hips themselves, the subtle sensuousness of their easy roll. *Follow me.*

He shuts the door behind us and steers me with a harsh grip above my elbow to stand in front of the bed, littered with the objects that swirled around my head all through dinner. Have they been occupying his mind as well?

His breath is hot in my ear as he bends down behind me. "Are you wet already, little bird?"

If I hadn't been before, his words would be enough to make me so. The low, insinuating softness of them masks something lusciously ominous and it strikes a chord inside of me.

"Yes, master."

"I could see your mind wandering while we ate. Did you figure it out? All the terrible things I'm going to do to you?"

I swallow hard because yes, I've conjured a hundred scenarios in the past hour or so but I know whatever he's dreamed up for me is going to be better than my imagination. He's quite creative and I wonder how he has all this time to think of me. His days are filled with prayer and work. Yet somehow he's planned this experience for us, and I'm grateful. "I have some ideas, master."

"I'm sure you do. Your mind is rarely quiet, is it Tzipporah?"

I shake my head, his beard rasping against the soft skin behind my ear and then his hand is at my throat, trapping me against him. "Answer me."

"No, master."

That's one of the things I like best about these times of ours together: how he's able to mute the thoughts that nag at me day and night. When we're with each other this way, all ideas are gone as if he's chased them away. If anyone could, it's Elan when he's being fierce as he is in here.

"I'm going to silence all that noise. The only thing you're going to be thinking of is me. Your only concern is pleasing me. Do you understand?"

"Yes, master."

"Keep your eyes on the bed," he instructs, and I

don't dare disobey. Then he strips me, removing layer upon layer until my tichels are the only things left. He unwinds them, disentangling the fine silk that's been wrapped intricately around my hair. When it's set free, he finger-combs it from root to tips, separating the strands and lifting some of them over my shoulders to drape over my breasts, the dark auburn curls drifting over my pale skin.

"So pretty," he says. "My beautiful wife."

His simple words make me feel beautiful. Desired.

"Bend over."

Yes.

I step forward and lean down until I can place my palms on the edge of the bed. The posture sends feelings of lust and vulnerability through me, and that's before his hand connects with my behind.

The impact forces a small noise from me. Not so much pain as of surprise, but yes, there's a sensual sting as well. Why I find the bite of pain so intensely erotic, I couldn't say. But I do. I so do. He continues to spank me as my eyes drift between the implements on the bed, fanning the coals of my smoldering desire for him into low flames that match the heated ache on my behind.

That's when he picks up the hairbrush.

The first impact makes me gasp, the broad head making contact with already sensitized flesh. He works me up steadily, hitting harder and harder until my cheeks are on fire and tears are pooling in my eyes. But I haven't stood up, haven't tried to cover myself. I've breathed through the pain and relished it, given myself over to him.

The blows stop and he leans over me, threading the fingers of one of his hands through mine.

"Good. My good girl."

He takes my wrists in his hands, gathering them behind my back and urges me to upright. When he's made sure I'm able to stand on my own, he guides me to the foot of the bed and reaches for a pillow that he drops on the floor.

"On your knees."

I kneel up, not sitting back on my heels, and tense for another hiding. Instead, he brushes my hair. Not like a man who doesn't understand these things, but starting at the bottom with small strokes and working out the tangles until he can drag the bristles from scalp to the ends without snagging on anything. So thoughtful, my Elan.

When my hair's been tamed to his satisfaction, he leaves me on my knees and reaches for a large hank of rope. I watch as he stands on the bed to unscrew what I thought was a cap on an unused light fixture and threads the rope through some kind of attachment point in the ceiling, leaving the thick cord dangling to the ground.

Then he takes up the large ring and affixes it to the ropes perhaps a foot above my head. He slides me, along with the pillow, to just under the contraption he's rigged and when I'm in place, unfurls one of the smaller bundles of rope and gathers my hair at the crown of my head.

It feels as though he threads the whole mass of it

through the ring and then there's a tug and a fall of hair down my back, as if he's using the ring as a pulley. Keeping tension in my scalp, he winds the narrower rope around the folded hair. He doesn't stop there though. There's more gentle tugging and then my hair's off my back again. More winding of rope and the sensation of a decisive tie off.

I can barely look up at him when he stands in front of me, my hair anchored as it is, but I can just see his face. He's completely absorbed by his task. With more rope, he winds quick, thick cuffs around my wrists and attaches them to the ring above my head, fashions a shelf of several layers of rope beneath my breasts—the better to display them—and uses more to attach canes to my knees and ankles, holding them apart.

The bondage has me completely helpless and exposed, rendering my insides into a quivering mass of desire. I have to refrain from rocking my hips and the tension in my scalp is a good reminder. *Don't move.*

Now that I'm staked out like a butterfly pinned in a specimen box, he reaches between my legs and strokes my clit for a few beats before diving his fingers further back and almost, but not quite inside me.

"You're soaking wet, little bird. You like being bound and helpless for me? You like being spanked?"

"Yes, master."

The confession makes my face heat and I want to look away, but the grip of his fingers hard on my jaw and the rope in my hair make it impossible.

"We're not done yet. You think I bound you up so

pretty just to admire you? No. Oh, no."

He strokes between my legs some more, seeming to know just how I like to be touched, precisely how to drive me crazy. He pushes me to the breaking point where I'm panting and straining to come and then backs off. "Not so fast. I've been looking forward to this and I'm going to take my time with you."

Leaving me in my bonds, he walks over to the bed where the clamps and a single cane are waiting. Apparently it's time to be hurt and my body warms and softens in anticipation. I crave this as much as I did before I could really have it. Who knew I could covet something more when it's mine than when it was out of my grasp?

He pockets some of the clamps and hefts the cane. Rattan. Not that it's heavy, but with his force behind it, it will be deliciously severe.

Standing before me, he surveys his prize, helpless and waiting for him, soaking wet and desperate. He's studying me, fixing his plans, or perhaps just torturing me with the wait. Then he kneels in front of me, still dwarfing me with his bulk, and puts down the cane before pulling a clamp from his pocket. He cups one of my breasts, kneads it until a sound escapes me and then toys with my nipple: pinching, pulling, rolling until he's satisfied. That's when he applies the clamp, the pressure biting into me so hard I yelp.

He cradles my face in his hand, thumb pressing into my cheek and forcing me to meet his gaze. "You're okay, Tzipporah. You can take it. Just breathe through it. You're going to do this for me."

I can, and his stern but encouraging gaze makes me believe I will. Doing as he says, I breathe, following the rise and fall of his broad shoulders, pinning my lifebreath to his. Soon, the screeching pain is fading to a dull roar.

"Good girl. See, I told you that you could do it. You have to trust me."

"Yes, master."

"I think you do. But it's still scary sometimes? I'll help you. I'm not going to make you do it alone."

His promise fortifies me when he pulls out another clamp and repeats the process on the other side. When they're both on, I'm more aware of my breasts. They feel swollen, tight, like the most obvious part of me, and oh, does that ever turn me on.

He strokes between my legs some more and it doesn't take long before I'm on the edge. But instead of letting me come, he takes more clamps from his pockets and shows them to me. "You're a smart girl, I bet you can guess where these are going."

I can and it scares me. He must see the alarm on my face because he pets me and soothes me, tells me I'm doing so well and he's so pleased with me. And then there's tightness and pressure on my labia, pinching. I suck air through my teeth as my eyes water but he talks me through it, encourages my breath, rubs the side of my ribcage.

"There's my sweet little bird. You're fragile, but so strong."

So I bear it until like the other ones, the bite fades and turns more into a throb. We've got to be close to finished. How much more can he ask of me? But then I remember the last cane. That's how much more.

He picks it up, swishes it through the air a few times and my heart beats harder. Getting down on one knee to my side, he wraps an arm around me so that my upper arms are braced against it. He has enough play for a decent swing but he won't be able to put his full force behind the blows, and I can steady myself against him so I don't pull too hard on my hair.

"Pick a number between one and twenty."

Oh, I hate this game. Forcing me to choose. He's so very wicked. I won't pick a low number because I don't want to disappoint him but I can't pick too high because I'm afraid. Before I can entirely psych myself out, I blurt, "Twelve."

"Mmm." His noise of acknowledgement doesn't give me much to work with, but I don't have long to think about it because the first stripe is landing across my behind, a defined line of pain. And I know by now that he wants me to count for him, thank him.

"One. Thank you, master."

And on it goes, line after line, hurt after hurt, tallying the strikes and expressing my gratitude. The strange thing is, I really am grateful. Thankful for him allowing me to be this way without disdain, for giving this to me freely and even joyfully. I thank Hashem, too, for sending me this man with whom I can share this. With whom I'm able to create these moments of wholeness and abandon in a life otherwise fraught with fear that I'll never be good enough for anyone.

I choke out eleven and he leans into me. Talks low in my ear. "Beg me for it, Tzipporah. Ask me to hurt you. Plead with me to hit you harder, make you suffer."

I'm so wet between my legs I can barely stand it, the pain ratcheting up my desire and making me crave him. The clamps have been jolted with every strike, reminding me anew of their presence and I'm practically out of my mind. So it's no surprise I do as he asks and babble the words frantically.

"Please, master. I need more. Hit me, bruise me. I want to feel this for days. Leave your marks on me. Make it hurt. I want to hurt for you. Please."

The cane falls across my flesh for the last time, this strike crossing the ones he's already made. He's hit me so hard I cry out without wanting to. There's nothing to do but scream. And cry. The tears I've been choking back finally spill and I start to bawl, the sobs racking my body.

It's such a relief. It's over, but I've done it. I've made him happy and in return, he's set me free, given me permission to fall completely and utterly apart.

He murmurs small, gruff words while he holds me, the sounds of the Yiddish soothing precisely because I can't understand and for the moment I give up trying. I haven't made much of an effort to learn because not so many people in my community speak it, not like in the Hasidic neighborhoods. In fact, it might be only the Kleins and a couple of the other more conservative families who use it and then not often. I've heard Elan speak it with his family, especially his brothers, but he doesn't usually use it around me. I'm glad he's chosen to now.

After I've calmed, he starts to untie me. It takes a long time because he's doing most of it single-handedly, keeping my slumped body against him so there's not too much weight on my scalp or my shoulders. When I'm finally free, he picks me up and lays me on the bed.

I find the lace edges of the bedspread easily though my eyes are closed. Curling my fingers around the side, I stroke weakly at them, needing to touch, needing to hold something solid.

"Are you with me, Tzipporah? Can you tell me?"

"Mmm."

"I need more than that."

Demanding man. I don't think I can open my eyes and talk at the same time, so I choose speech. "Still here. Want more."

Of course he laughs at me. I don't mind. He spreads my legs wide and then his fingers are inside me. I sigh because the penetration feels so good. It makes me want more. But instead of stripping and pressing inside of me, he releases the clamps and holy—

"Sugar!"

My modified curse makes him laugh again. This time I open my eyes to see his face, the streak of white teeth surrounded by his beard, the way wrinkles form at the sides of his eyes. "That hurts, does it?"

"You know it does."

My brain must be scrambled indeed, because that is not an appropriate response. Nor does he think so; I get a slap to the side of my breast for my insolence. "Try again."

"Yes, master."

"Better."

And then he's pulling the clamps from my nipples, licking and suckling away the pain from the rush of blood. It hurts, but it feels good and everything is starting to register as just *feeling*. I want him to make me feel more.

"Elan, I want you inside me. Please."

He could slap me again, perhaps a pinch. It's not my place to make demands. Instead, he stands, strips off his clothes and folds them. I watch him, the flex of his muscles as he performs this simple task and I suddenly want to see him at work so very badly. How ruthless and brutal would he seem hacking and tearing at huge pieces of meat? My great bear of a husband, who can be so gentle as he settles himself between my legs and leans over to ease inside of me.

When he's sure I can take him easily, the momentary gentleness is over and he ravages me, pounding inside, the motion slamming my abused behind into the bed. With every thrust it hurts anew, the fire set all over again as if he's striking match after match and using my flesh as tinder.

I clutch at his back, my fingers digging into him. I need so badly to hold onto something and he's my only shelter in the storm. Soon I'm whimpering because I need yet another release. I believe he'll fulfill his responsibility and give it to me, urging me with his words.

"Yes, little bird. I want to see you fly."

I do, my whole body pure sensation as I come apart underneath him. My nails dig into him as he drives his way to his own release, my cries sending him higher until he goes rigid above me and I feel the pulse of his orgasm inside me.

After our breathing returns to an approximation of normal, he rolls off me, nudging my shoulder so he can lie alongside me. He lifts an arm to look at the side of his ribcage and snorts.

"Look what you've done to me, you little brute."

The streaky red marks my nails have left on his skin make me giggle. "It only seems fair after what you've done to me, you hulking savage."

I roll onto my stomach so he can see the marks he made, knowing they'll darken into bruises over the next few days. For now the livid red welts will please him. I expect him to stroke them, perhaps pinch or tweak them, but instead I hear the grind of a drawer opening and then he's rubbing a cream onto the marks.

"Arnica," he replies to my startled noise. I settle into his caretaking, relishing the kindness of the act, soaking up affection where I can get it.

CHAPTER FIVE

W E'VE BEEN MARRIED for almost a month so it shouldn't have surprised me when I woke up eleven days ago to my period starting. But somehow, it had.

I'd stood in the bathroom, wondering what exactly I should say. I had to tell him and the idea was mortifying—*I barely know this man and I have to tell him it's that time of the month? Ugh*. But not telling him would've been so much worse. Then he wouldn't know to treat me as niddah: no touching, no passing things between us, no seeing those private parts only he's entitled to.

So I'd done it when we'd passed in the kitchen, him loading his breakfast dishes in the dishwasher before heading off to the shul for morning services and me putting on the kettle for my tea. After our arms nearly brushed, I'd worked up the nerve. "I'm bleeding. You can't—"

He'd taken a step back from me and I'd felt the disconnect right away. The one bond we'd solidified over the past two weeks broken. And as if the symbolism hadn't been enough, when I'd come home that night it had been to the one large bed separated into two, divided by our nightstands in the middle.

When I'd been married to Brooks, I'd romanticized the idea of being niddah. A time when husband and wife aren't permitted to each other. To live with one another, passing by, watching, talking, wanting but not being able to touch. How inflammatory would sex be after you've been kept from it for twelve days?

But as some things do, being niddah has turned out to be far less enjoyable than I'd imagined. For me, the past eleven days have been miserable. I hadn't realized exactly how dependent my relationship with Elan is on kink and sex. Apparently it's all we have.

Not that he was particularly talkative or affectionate before, but there were always moments of kindness, of intimacy, of connection. Flirtation. Now I don't have even those to sustain me. Our physical closeness had apparently been greasing the wheels of our otherwise stiff and awkward interactions.

I don't think it's my imagination that he's avoiding me more than usual. Or that I've been scolded far more frequently and in a way that's far from fun. And here we go again.

"You can't hand me that, Tzipporah."

My eyes water at the fatigued censure in his voice. Right, yes. I have to put it down before he can pick it up.

"Sorry," I mutter as I set the glass down on the counter, color high in my cheeks. How long is this going to take me to learn?

"Don't be sorry. You'll learn."

But I am sorry, I'm sorry about all of it. I'm frustrated with myself for not being able to remember all of these things and his annoyance at having to remind me of the rules is clear, which only serves to make me feel worse. I feel like a child. A badly behaved, stupid child. I've been on the verge of tears for days and I don't think I can hold them in for another minute. But I have to. I don't want him to see me cry, not if he hasn't beaten the tears out of me.

After a dinner we eat in silence with an empty glass in between our places to remind us of my status, and during which I begin to fear that I've made an enormous and humiliating mistake, I excuse myself to my office and take up my phone.

"Bina, can I come over?"

WHEN SHE GREETS me at the door, her face folds into deep sympathy. "Oh, Tzipporah, come in, come in."

She shows me to a small sitting room at the back of the house away from where her husband and half a dozen other men are arguing some finer point of gemora in the living room. When we sit on a small couch together, I start to cry.

Face in my hands, the tears gather in my palms.

"I'm so lonely, Bina. He won't talk to me. And I screw up all the time. I feel so stupid and he's so angry at me."

She pets me as I sob and I bury my head into her shoulder. She smells of blown out candles and cosmetics and it's so very comforting.

"There," she says, drawing away to hand me a tissue. "It can't be as bad as all that."

"It is," I insist petulantly. But her steady gaze tells me she's not entirely buying my story. It is possible I'm being a titch dramatic. "Fine. But it's pretty bad."

"Tell me then, now that you're not in hysterics."

"He barely says a word to me."

"Well, Elan's never been much with words. He can give an excellent dvar torah if he's called upon but he's not like them." She gestures with her chin down the hall, indicating the men's voices rising over one another, an argumentative mash of Hebrew and English.

"I know but without the—" My mouth snaps shut and my cheeks heat. Bina's old enough to be my mother and I would *not* talk about this with my mother.

"You can say sex to me. I have eight children and I used to be a kallah teacher you know." Yes, I know. Her children all live in the neighborhood with children of their own and I know she used to lead the classes for brides-to-be. Regardless, I have to tone down the words.

"Without being together in the bedroom, we don't have conversation. Except for transactions. *I'll be home at six. We're having a meat dinner.* You know. And then he yells at me."

She raises an eyebrow. "He yells at you?"

I purse my lips, because technically no. Truth be

told, I can't imagine Elan yelling. It would probably shake the earth if he ever really lost his temper. All of Brooklyn would know. "Well, no. But it *feels* like yelling."

"Is he cruel to you?" The silk trail of her scarves shift as she tips her head, the ends drifting over her shoulder.

Cruel? He doesn't ridicule me, doesn't call me names and I can't let her think anything remotely like that about Elan. He's a good man, he just—

"No, of course not. It just makes me feel terrible that I can't please him. And he gets frustrated with me."

"It's hard on you both. It takes time to learn these things. Everyone makes mistakes. I've been doing this for as long as you've been alive, I'm a rabbi's wife, and I'm still not perfect. Close…" She winks and I have to smile, the expression probably pathetic on my tear-stained face. "…but not quite. Elan's had years of practice."

Yes, with his perfect Orthodox wife who I'm sure never messed up as frequently as I do. It's not often that I get stabs of jealousy of Rivka, though I suspect Elan will never love me as he loved her. I know, too, his brothers and their wives adored her, not like me who they seem to tolerate. Yes, I've been welcome in their homes, but they always talk to me as if I'm not one of them.

Maybe other people wouldn't notice, but I did my dissertation on how insular religious groups speak with outsiders. I recognize how their speech patterns change when they're talking to me instead of each other. How they use fewer Hebrew and Yiddish words and frequently translate the ones they do use. As if I haven't been a part of this community for years, as if I don't have more Hebrew and Aramaic than most of the women because of my field of study.

Keeping niddah though, this is one area where my shortcomings aren't imagined. They're very real and I'm sure I compare very poorly indeed. Yes, I know Elan is perfect in this observance as I've been reminded over and over for the past eleven days. He's had half a lifetime of practice.

"And you've had none. You're too hard on yourself. Maybe too much of a perfectionist, yes? You're so used to being head of the class and in this, you're not. It won't make him love you any less."

Love me? "I don't even think he likes me."

Finds me attractive, yes, enjoys beating and fucking me, sure, but otherwise, he seems to be mostly perplexed by his odd wife and her strange ways.

"What makes you say that?"

"He won't even talk to me!"

She shakes her head. "Silly girl. Did you ever think you might intimidate him?"

"Why on earth would Elan be afraid of me? He could snap me like a twig." Nearly has, come to think of it, but I liked it.

"That's true. But you're a fancy college professor. You use all these big words and walk around with your head in the clouds all day. Why would you want to talk to a butcher?"

"But Elan is so smart. He runs his business, he's had

so much more learning than I have." It perhaps was a bit sneaky of me, but I'd hid in the hallway and listened to him and Moyshe during their chavrusa session. I know more gemora than most Orthodox women because I've studied it in school but I'll probably never catch up to my husband who's been studying these things nearly every day for his entire life. I admire him for it. "And it's not like religious studies is astrophysics. He would understand my work. Even if I were a rocket scientist, he could learn. I know he could."

Her mouth spreads into a kind smile. "Maybe he doesn't know you think so. He's not like you, doesn't wear his heart and insecurities on his sleeve. And having to leave yeshiva to take over the business... You don't think he wonders why they chose him to give up his studies?"

I've never thought much about why it was Elan who took over the butcher shop instead of Moyshe or Dovid but it sounds like it wasn't entirely his choice, even if he's happy now. That *is* something to think about. Now I feel guilty on top of everything else. And because as Bina's said, my emotions aren't exactly subtle, she pats my hand.

"Don't fret. Just think about it. And here, let's have some tea before you go home to your husband."

AN HOUR LATER, I let myself back into our apartment. The light is on in the dining room. I'm tempted to head straight to my office as I usually do and stay there because there are some things I need to do for class tomorrow. But with Bina's advice echoing in my head, I pick up a notebook and a couple of textbooks and bring them into where he's bent over a ledger on the table. He looks up at the squeak of the floor that signals my entrance.

"You're home. Good." Am I imagining a hint of relief in his voice? As if he were worried I wouldn't come back, or was concerned because I was out late? I let myself cling to it because I want to believe he'd care if something happened to me instead of being relieved that something had fixed his mistake.

"Yes. I'm sorry I didn't call."

He shrugs and goes back to his work, his pen held just over the page he's working on. I stutter-step because my confidence has been shaken by his seeming indifference. But Bina would say that's all it is. Pretend. He really does care. So I find it within myself to take the several more steps to the table and sit, laying my things out at my place.

He glances up, his forehead wrinkling with the movement. I hope he isn't upset that I'm in here with him instead of shutting myself in my office with my modern art on the walls, pop music streaming from the small speakers I plug into my laptop.

I open my notebook and flip to a marked page in my book, as if we do this all the time, work together at the same table.

After a minute of staring at me, he goes about his

business and returns to his rows of numbers. I try to concentrate on the pages in front of me, but I end up reading them over and over though I've taught this material time and again. It shouldn't be this difficult to come up with a lesson on the similarities of women's clothing across Orthodox branches of Christianity, Judaism and Islam. When I just can't stand it anymore, I look up.

"What—what are you working on?"

He looks up from under heavy brows as if he's not totally sure I'm speaking to him, though we're alone in the house. He even looks over his shoulder. The movement is comical but I keep my laugh tucked away. I don't want to embarrass him. He won't talk to me if I embarrass him.

Besides, I really am curious. He usually reserves the evenings for religious studies, taking down one or another of the seforim that line the bookshelves in the living room and poring over it. For him to be looking at something for work is unusual. I hope it's not an indication that something is wrong.

"I'm double-checking the numbers on our last shipment of lamb. We ran out today. We almost never run out. I wanted to make sure it was because we sold more than usual, not because not as much got delivered."

I nod. "Does Reuven help you with that?"

"He does, but he does everything on the computer and shows it to me like it's supposed to make sense. It's not that I don't trust him, I just…I like to see it on paper."

"I get it." I show him my notebook, my handwriting scrawled across the lines. "I love my laptop, but I remember things better if I write them down instead of type. Same reason I get hardcopy textbooks instead of digital. The information just sticks better somehow."

He regards me curiously, and then turns back to his own work. My shoulders slump because I'd hoped to get more than two minutes of conversation out of my efforts. But baby steps, right? I can keep trying, keep prying him open like a long-buried treasure chest with a rusty latch. My gathering of mental lock-picking tools is interrupted by Elan clearing his throat.

"And you. What is that?" His question sounds a little edgy, like he's afraid of the answer. Does he think I'm going to launch into a dissertation he won't understand?

"I'm making notes for my lecture tomorrow. We're talking about religious clothing. Head coverings in particular."

His gaze darts to my scarves and then away again. "What about them?"

I shrug, feeling awkward. It's easy to talk about this in front of a lecture hall full of students, so much harder across the table from my husband. But I'm so thrilled he's asked, I stammer an answer.

"People think Christianity and Islam and Judaism are so different. But really, we have so much in common. Hijab, veils and wimples, tichels and sheitels, they're very much the same. It's one of my favorite classes."

Examples so concrete help students make connections and it's usually one of the times I can see something click inside their heads. And a few of them, though they've been staring at my covered head since the beginning of the semester, will actually work up the nerve to ask me about it after class. I don't mind their self-conscious inquiries and some of the girls even ask me where I get my scarves. They think they're beautiful.

Elan asks me a few more questions and his shy interest delights me. Bina is so smart and I'll have to call her and tell her so tomorrow. An hour or so later, finished with my notes and feeling decently prepared for my classes the next day, I fold up my books and heft them into my arms. It's my turn to work up some nerve. Again.

"I—" I huff, annoyed with myself. I can only hope that someday we'll be able to have a conversation without so much horrible stuttering. "I go to the mikveh tomorrow."

It's embarrassing, yes, informing him of what I've always thought of as a private matter, but the way his eyes light up, I don't feel so embarrassed anymore. No, the heat rising in my cheeks is more a result of thinking about what's going to happen tomorrow when I get home.

I'D BEEN ANXIOUS to get to the mikveh because it meant I was that much closer to being with Elan again, but now that I find myself here, I'm not in a hurry to leave. It's a peaceful, quiet sanctuary and amidst all the busyness and anxiety of my life right now, it's nice to be in the company of women. I feel a bit like an imposter here, but it's because I'm unpracticed like any recently married woman, not because this was knowledge I was supposed to have acquired through a lifetime and…haven't.

The attendant shows me to one of the preparation rooms that I remember from the day of my wedding. There's less pomp and circumstance now but I go through the motions: taking off the nail polish that's been chipping off for a week because I forget to deal with it, clipping my nails, brushing out my hair, taking off makeup and all my jewelry. I take a shower, too, washing my hair, combing it out hoping to remove any loose strands before I go into the small pool, shaving and making sure any stray hairs are rinsed from my body, thinking of how Elan might touch me now that he's permitted again.

As I perform my ablutions, I have to shake myself out of my daydreams. I'm supposed to be thinking spiritual, mystical thoughts, not about the dirty, dirty things I'll be doing with my husband later. But I can't imagine I'm the first woman to have sex fantasies in here. Not even close.

When I've finally divested myself of all earthly dirt and grime, I ring the attendant to let her know I'm ready. After she's checked my hands and feet for nail polish and any speck of dirt, she guides me, clad in my robe, down the short hall.

I know it shouldn't matter, but I love that I get to go to a pretty mikveh, all shiny and new. It's only been open for a few years and it's all tiles and marble. The lighting is soft and it doesn't look so different from the spas my mother frequents.

The first time I was here, I cried. It's a very powerful feeling, being connected to generations of women who have done this for thousands of years. The trappings might have changed but the ritual is the same. And especially now with the growing rift between me and my mom, it seems more important than ever to have this shared sense of feminine history and bonding.

The attendant helps me out of my robe, holding it in front of her so she doesn't see my naked entrance into the warm water. And as I walk down the seven steps that curl into the pool in a spiral, the difficulties of the past twelve days melt away. I recall Bina's kind words and I think of everything that called me to this life and this community, and yes, how wonderful it will be to be with Elan again in the way we seem to connect best.

It's going to take time, probably the rest of my life. I'm always going to be a ba'alat teshuva. But this feels right to me in a way my old life never did, even if it's not easy. When I reach the bottom of the stairs, I let the warm water surround and comfort me. I say the blessing for immersion and then sink entirely into the water, feeling as though my worries and mistakes are washing away.

I submerge myself three times, each time feeling cleaner, stronger, and more optimistic. I am one among many and there are so many people who support me in this. Taking a breath when I come up out of the pool for the last time, I don't feel like crying. I feel joy.

At the top of the stairs, the attendant helps me into my robe and I go back to the changing room to get dressed and dry my hair. Perhaps it's my imagination, but when I check my reflection in the mirror, my face isn't worn and weary, I don't look enervated from the stresses of the past nearly two weeks. I look radiant.

I take my time getting dressed and ready. As I'm winding my hair up to tuck inside the scarves, I think of Elan unwinding them. How he'll take his time though surely he's as eager for my body as I am for his.

BLISSED OUT AND dreamy, I practically float up the stairs to our apartment and it takes me a few tries to open the door. When I do, Elan's big body is in the hallway, blocking the light from the dining room. If I didn't know it was him, I might be afraid. Especially when he sets upon me and pushes me up against the door I just closed behind me.

My back hits the wood as he grips my neck, tipping up my chin. "I've been waiting for you."

"I'm sorry?"

He shakes his head. "For days, Tzipporah, I've been waiting for you."

His dark eyes seem darker, like if I fall into them I might never be able to crawl out. At this moment, I never want to. I've been craving his touch so badly and now I can have it.

"I've been waiting for you too."

He kisses me then—his mouth devouring mine, his hand that's not at my throat groping me anywhere he can reach, reminding me with every aggressive squeeze, every painful pinch that I belong to him. It's not long before he's dragging me toward the bedroom.

"Elan!" I'm laughing because I'm practically tripping over myself as he bundles me down the hall. *This.* This is what I've wanted.

"Dangerous," he mutters, as if he's just realized there's no way I can keep up with his long strides and he's going to make me fall. I think he's going to slow down, but instead he reaches for me and as if I weigh nothing, hefts me over his shoulder and carries on, barely pausing.

I'm now in full-on delighted giggle fits, which earns me a very firm smack to my behind that makes me yelp.

"Quiet, please."

His request almost makes me laugh harder, the politeness of the words juxtaposed with the demanding gravelly tone. But I find it somewhere inside me to honor his wish. I can be quiet.

After closing our bedroom door, he sets me down and his eyes rake over me, his gaze so hot he might set my very clothes on flashfire that would burn them clean off my body, leaving my skin unscathed. Instead he pushes me up against this door too and the impact sends a jolt of desire through me. What is it about being handled this way that makes me so hot?

Who cares?

He kisses me again and this time, he doesn't stop at groping, but strips my clothes as he goes. Soon I'm naked and my hair is flowing down my back. He pulls away and pins me to the door at arm's length with a hand at my throat, as if he won't be able to stop devouring me if he doesn't break contact, but can't quite bring himself to cease touching me entirely.

"You're not to speak. I want control of your very voice and you're going to give it to me. You're going to make noise, I promise you, but no words after you've said yes. Do you understand me?"

No words. To have something so strongly entwined with my entire personality taken away... Words are who I am. They're what I do. Without words, I have no livelihood, I have no worth. To have them stolen—panic rises inside me. But no. He wouldn't *steal* them, wouldn't take without my permission. He's asking and I can say yes or no. This will either be insanely hot or a massive struggle. Perhaps a mixture of both and there's only one way to find out.

"Yes, master."

His pupils dilate with lust and then he grabs me by the hips and spins me to face the door, then pushes me to my knees. "Stay."

I wait, trying to be patient while I listen to the sounds of him moving about the room. In time, he's gathering my hair into a ponytail at the top of my head and cinching it with rope. I think he might braid the strand through as he's done several times before, but instead it feels like he's tying knot after knot, a swift wrap followed by a decisive tug. Like he's fashioning a tube of rope around my hair. When he's finished, he pulls me to stand and presses me against the door, anchoring me by the trailing strands to the door frame. Then he wraps quick rope cuffs around my wrists and ties them to anchor points above my head.

My cheek is pressed against the cool wood that quickly grows warm from the heat of my body. My shoulders drop. I'm not responsible for my speech and now I'm not responsible for my movements either. They're his to control.

"Eyes closed." Now my sight is his, too.

He leaves me again briefly, but then he's back, crowding me with his bulk though not touching me. I expect some kind of impact because the spanking—oh, how we both enjoy the spanking, but there's a gentle drift of something across my back. Strands of—suede? I can't quite tell and I know better than to turn around and look.

"Have you ever been flogged, little bird?"

I open my mouth to answer, but I remember his directive just in time: no words.

So I nod.

"Good girl, remembering your instructions. Did you enjoy it?"

I bite my lip in indecision. Because I hadn't. Brooks didn't know what he was doing, and I don't think the cheap flogger he'd ordered online from some kind of novelty store had helped any. But I think I could enjoy it. It's frustrating that he's taken my words so I can't explain any of this. I'll answer his question honestly though. I shake my head as well as I can.

The caress of the strands over my skin pauses and I wonder if he'll stop. I don't want him to stop. I'd beg him to try because I think it would be different with him. But it's more of a hiccup than a full stop and the gentle stroking continues.

It lulls me into a trance although something inside me crackles with anticipation. He didn't string me up like this to be gentle with me. That's when the strands leave my skin and the first blow falls. Still gentle, I might call it a tease. A taste. I want more. I want to gorge myself on sensation now that I'm allowed to break my fast from touch.

He works up, the strands falling ever harder and it's not so long before I'd call them blows. Impact. Force. At one particularly hard strike, I gasp. He grips the back of my neck, his thumb rubbing over the juncture with my shoulder.

"Is this better?"

His question is soft but I hear it because I'm straining for any word from him. I nod. Yes, this is what I'd hoped for when I'd asked Brooks, heart in my throat, to try.

"Good."

And then he hits me harder. And harder. So hard it feels as though he's beating the air out of my body. I have to suck oxygen into my lungs between impacts and I love it. I'm making noise with every whack of the flogger but never do I use my words. I don't have to use my words because he knows. When it stops, I want to cry, I want to ask for more but I can't so I wait, hoping, too, he knows I can take more.

I'm tempted to make an inquisitive noise—as if I think he'd answer me—but I'm stopped by a thin, sharp sting on my shoulder blade.

"Ah!" It's a wheedling burn that lingers, growing hot after the initial impact and fading too slowly. What the hell was that? Then there's another and another. He's making a pattern along the plane of my upper back. I breathe through it, only making small pained whimpers now that I've gotten a handle on how to process the sensation. I wouldn't call it easy, but definitely manageable. I can do this.

But then it changes. He's struck the lower side of my ribs with the evil little tool and it makes me cry out. He balances it out with a strike on the other side and I try to pull away but I can't because I'm fixed to the door by my hair and my hands.

"Stop moving or I'll bind your ankles too."

The temptation to disobey is real because I think it would be easier to bear if he took that from me as well, but I don't want to disappoint him. So I still my feet, pretending there are roots from my soles growing into the floor and holding me fast, that the shallow stalks anchoring me could twine with his somewhere in the earth. It makes it the barest bit easier to endure what feel like tiger stripes of pain he's clawing down my ribs.

It stops again and he presses his front to my back, pushing me into the door, containing me. The force steadies me and I pin my draws and exhales of air to his.

"There you go. I want control over even your breath." The idea should terrify me but it doesn't. It lets me sink further into his hold. When I've calmed to his satisfaction, he murmurs, "Just a little more for me. You can do it."

I nod, because for him I can. I want to. The endorphins flooding my system help of course, but he's the one who's given that to me, knowing I'd need them for what he wants from me. The care and consideration he lavishes on me during these times makes me ache, swells my heart.

That's when the first tiny little bolt of lightning falls on my arm. *Shit.* I've gotten so good at not swearing—even in my head, for the most part—but he's driven me to this. He works his way toward my wrist and with every shrill impact, it hurts more. Maybe it's because he's getting further away from my core that it feels more dangerous? He stops at the middle of my forearm when I'm just shy of tears but heavy of breath and I feel triumphant. He won't go any further because I'm positive whatever he's using on me is going to leave marks.

He praises me in soft, gentle words and I swim in them, soaking in his pleasure. Then he unhooks one of my wrists from above the door. We must be finished if he's releasing me. But he doesn't undo any of my other bondage. Instead, he extends my arm away from my body, not touching the wall. Exposed.

"You took ten on your right arm and we can't have

you lopsided. Ten on this side and then we're done. You don't need to count but at the end, you'll thank me."

I have to earn my voice back. The thought makes me swallow convulsively but I'm up for a challenge so when he asks if I'm ready, I nod.

I didn't think it was possible but it hurts more on this side. Maybe because I don't have the comfort of the rope binding me, maybe because I don't have the support of the wall. Or perhaps it's just some bizarre mindfucky thing that, unlike with the other arm, which was bound and held fast for him to torture, this is very much my choice, down to my core, and I'm still offering up my body to be hurt.

I count the burning slashes in my head and make it to four before I start to cry. The tears roll hot and fast down my cheeks, but I don't move my arm. By the time it's over, my chest is heaving against the door and I'm pressing my face into the wood, seeking comfort, clenching and unclenching my fists, as if anything will help.

But the only thing that helps is when it stops and Elan's big body is against mine. He circles my wrist in his hand and pulls it toward my shoulder, bending my elbow until it's folded close against my body like a resting bird's wing.

He holds me while I wear out my tears, crooning kind things to me in words that are foreign but comforting. I wish my understanding of Yiddish were better because it's possible he's speaking poetry in my ear, but all I can glean are fleeting basic words: good, beautiful, mine.

Pinning me to the door with his hard, naked body, he undoes the rest of my bonds. I'm glad he didn't tie my ankles because I think I might collapse if he had to let me go to untie them. When he's done, he hefts me up and presses my back to the door, insinuating his hips between my thighs and guiding himself inside.

I sigh. After feeling so much like a disappointment, so lacking on every level, I feel whole now. Wanted. Complete. It's possible that this feels so good because I've felt so very bad, a crest to the emotional trough I've been wallowing in. I wouldn't wish for this level of desperation every month but I hope the pure delight welling inside me as I thread my fingers through his thick hair always remains. It's a privilege to experience this anew.

He's not gentle as he thrusts into me. My back and behind hit the door over and over and it brings the marks he's made alive. It doesn't quite register as pain though, more like feeling and the intensity is overwhelming. He's transformed me into pure sensation. I am so, so lucky.

"Thank you," I say in between thrusts. "Thank you, Elan. Thank you, master."

As if he's been cradling me in his hands and is now propelling me into the sky, his words create a current of air that carries me off. "Soar for me, Tzipporah. Take flight."

So I do.

CHAPTER SIX

A LITTLE OVER a week later, we're hosting our first Shabbos. Thus far, dinner has gone really well. I'm glad I took the day off even though I might have been close to a nervous breakdown for much of it while I was cooking because I was agonizingly conscious of not screwing up. It's one thing to eat a salad and leftovers when it's just me and Elan, as we've had to do a couple of times already, and my parents would probably be delighted if I served enchiladas or something—*she hasn't gone entirely off the deep end!*—but it would be a whole different matter to tell his parents I'd failed.

Elan seems to me a dutiful son. He's taken over the family business so his brothers could continue at yeshiva and Klein Brothers wouldn't have to close, after all. But sometimes it seems as though tensions between him and his parents run quite high. Maybe because he's not as rigid in his observance as they are? I can only hope it's not entirely to do with his decision to marry me.

I know I'm not their idea of a dream wife for their

son—I'm a ba'alat teshuva after all, there are no distinguished rabbis in my family, and they don't care that my grandfather was a well-known record producer. Elan's never shared with me the reasons he doesn't seem as close to his parents as Moyshe and Dovid do and I don't want to pry. It's not like I want to hash out the reasons for my own familial drift.

Speaking of...

"Z—Tzipporah," my father says, not bothering to contain his eye roll. He'll call me my chosen name but not without letting me know he doesn't like it. "It's late and your mother and I should be going."

What?

"But..." It's Shabbos. We'd invited them to stay and they'd agreed, if reluctantly. I cleaned the guestroom today, made the bed. Even bought flowers for the bureau. Delphinium, my mother's favorite. I know they think it's ridiculous, to not drive on Shabbos, but I was hoping they'd respect my feelings, if not my beliefs. Elan's parents will be horrified. "I thought you and Mom were going to stay."

"We were, but we're supposed to meet the Gilberts for dinner tomorrow evening and we won't make it in time if we wait until sundown tomorrow."

"But—" They hadn't mentioned dinner with the Gilberts when I invited them to have Shabbos with us over a week ago. Which means they either already had the plans with the Gilberts and always intended to leave early, or if they made the dinner plans after the fact, did it blithely, knowing it would upset me.

Elan rests a hand on my thigh under the table and leans over. "It's okay, Tzipporah. We offered a place for them to stay so they wouldn't have to break Shabbos. It's not your fault that they're choosing to. No one will hold you at fault. You've done your duty. Don't worry about it."

Disappointment and humiliation are making my throat tight, even though I know Elan is right and he's absolved me of any responsibility. It's their choice and we've done everything possible to make it comfortable for them to keep the Sabbath. It's not our fault they won't.

So I plaster on a tight smile in the face of Elan's parents' blatant disapproval. "Of course. But won't you stay for dessert?"

I don't expect them to say yes and they don't, bidding the Kleins good night. Tonight had been awkward, which I fully expected, but I'd thought all things considered it had gone pretty well. Until now.

I offer to walk my parents to the door, excusing myself from the table.

"Thank you for dinner," my mom says, shrugging on her coat. "We'll have to do it again sometime."

I can't help muttering a sulky, "Not on Shabbos."

"Don't be difficult," my father snaps, irritation flaring on his face. "We sat through hours of conversation with those people."

"*Those people* are my family now and you barely talked to them."

"What are we supposed to say to them, Zoe? They're

from a different planet."

"You only feel that way because you don't know them."

Not that I'm comfortable with Elan's parents by any stretch of the imagination, but they certainly don't deserve to be referred to as "those people." If my parents tried a little harder...

"Maybe next time you can come up to Avon?"

My mother's suggestion softens me but there's no way we'd be able to spend the weekend at my parents' home. They'd probably serve us ham and cheese omelets on Saturday morning. The very idea makes my insides knot up. It's been one thing to try to muddle through when it's just me, but to involve Elan and have my parents disregard his faith that way would be unacceptable.

"Maybe for Sunday brunch," I offer. "Sarah and Joel could come too."

I'd have to bring food and dishes for us, but that's fine. We could make it work. I'd like for my siblings and their families to meet Elan since they haven't yet. I bet they'd like him, given the chance, and the kids would adore him. I've watched him play with his nieces and nephews and the sight warmed my heart. But the frown on my mother's face tells me she's not interested in what she considers to be a consolation prize. "Maybe."

They bid me a good night and I stand with my back to the door after they've gone. It's nearly impossible, but I swear I hear a lone car start on the street outside our building. My face burns with mortification because surely the entire neighborhood knows that's my family, driving on Shabbos. As if they needed a reminder that I don't quite belong here.

Taking a few deep breaths, I prepare myself to face the Kleins again. Until my parents' untimely departure, I thought I'd earned at least a scrap of their approval. And I'm confident his father enjoyed my brisket, though he's lost most of his speech from the stroke and couldn't tell me so. He did help himself to thirds after all.

I head back to clear the table and when I've nearly reached the dining room, low voices in angry tones leak into the hallway, making me stop short. I should probably just walk in, but I'm curious. Elan keeps so much from me outside the bedroom that I can't help hope this might give me a glimpse into the man I call my husband.

"Where do you get these women, Elan?"

"Same place as Moyshe and Dovid got their wives. Exactly where I'm supposed to. From the shul. From the matchmakers who think they know better than everyone else and the bubbes who like nothing better than to see men and women married off. You want to argue with the rebbetzin? Be my guest."

"I don't appreciate your sarcasm." No, I can't imagine that his mother does. And for him to sound so short with her, he must be irritated indeed. "You know what I mean. First Rivka, and now this one. If I didn't know you spent the day watching her, I wouldn't trust that the food was kosher. I wasn't sure she was going to make it through the blessing. And her parents—" Her sentence is punctuated by a guttural sound of disgust.

I'm disappointed in my parents, too, but I don't want them sneered at. They may not share the same beliefs that I do, but they don't deserve scorn and I wish he would stand up for them. At the very least I want Elan to defend *me*. Tell them I stumbled through the blessing because I was so nervous, having to perform in front of everyone like some kind of trained monkey, knowing my recital would be critiqued. I want him to swear up and down that I've done everything right, that I'm trying so very hard. But all I get is a muttered, "The food is kosher."

And what kind of problem could they possibly have had with Rivka? As far as I can tell, she was the perfect Orthodox wife. Helped him with the business, kept their home, always acted appropriately and I'm sure never forgot any of the myriad rules because she probably learned them by osmosis in the womb. The embodiment of frum from birth. I don't particularly feel like hearing any more criticisms of either myself or Rivka, so I step back into the dining room.

"Would anyone like some rugelach?" The smile grows tight on my face and I have to grit my teeth to keep from screaming when the elder Kleins look at me with dubious expressions on their faces. "No dairy, I promise."

When his parents have gone, Elan helps me clean up. As I go up on tip-toes to put the final dish back in the cabinet, he comes up behind me, resting his hands on the countertops to my sides. I've been trapped. I set my heels on the ground and he moves closer until he's pressed against my back.

"Let's go to bed."

This is usually the point that I would grind my hips against the hardness pushing into me, but my libido has been completely squashed by disappointment. In my parents for not honoring their promises. In Elan for not standing up for me. We both know I'm not perfect but it wouldn't kill him to be more loyal. When we're alone I don't always feel like this marriage was a mistake, but when we're with other people, I constantly feel like a failure.

"I'm tired." He stiffens behind me and I feel a momentary pang of regret. We usually have sex on Shabbos and I'm refusing him.

He makes a gruff noise before taking a step back. "Of course. You worked very hard today."

I did. And it's still not good enough for you. For anyone.

He kisses my cheek, the soft scrape of his beard a familiar enticement that doesn't quite catch my desire. I squeeze my eyes shut because they've started to water and then he's gone.

As we fall asleep I don't seek out his body but lie curled up on my side facing the door. The symbolism doesn't require an advanced degree to interpret. There's an escape from this, a way out, and perhaps I should take it.

I'd thought marrying Elan would make me feel more a part of the community but instead I feel as though I'm being driven away. I shouldn't feel more alone living in the same house, sleeping in the same bed as a man than I did when I lived by myself, and yet... What have I done?

ON SATURDAY AFTER a long morning at services, I'm feeling brittle. I didn't sleep well last night, tossing and turning, falling into dreams where I was flying through dark woods. For some reason there were doors amongst the trees but all of them were closed. I'd fly into them at top speed but they wouldn't budge; I'd just end up dazed on the forest floor. Over and over. And then I'd seen it. A door that was open just a crack. So I'd slipped through the narrow opening toward the light and once I'd gotten through, I woke up.

We're at Moyshe's house, where we've been invited to spend the afternoon and evening. The thought of being around Elan's parents for the rest of the day makes me queasy but I'm not going to play sick. Elan is at the dining room table with some of the other men discussing the morning's services. The conversation is loud and argumentative and I'd wager half of it is in Hebrew and sprinkled with Yiddish for good measure. Rarely do I hear my husband's voice, but I catch snippets of it while I sit on the floor and play with some of my new nieces and nephews.

Of anyone in this family, I think the children like me best. Though they correct my mistakes too. I have a PhD in religious studies, have spent more than half my life learning about the beliefs and practices of faiths around the world. It's demoralizing to be told by a four-year-old that I'm doing Judaism wrong.

I've already been rebuffed for suggesting putting together a puzzle. Tamar had looked at me like I'd tried to hand her a cheesesteak before proposing we string beads instead. "Ima tied the knots at the end of the strings yesterday!"

Of course her mother would remember to do such things so her children could string beads on Shabbos. Perhaps it will be a good thing for any children Elan and I have to grow up in such an observant family. Then they'll never feel as out of place as I do. They won't face the same struggles. But the idea of my own children disdaining me because on a listless Saturday afternoon I try to give them Play-Doh or sort cards for a game is depressing.

Maybe I should've married another BT like most of the people I met at the outreach center and my seminary. A man like that could understand what it's like in a way Elan never will. And though I'm sure he'd correct me, perhaps it wouldn't sound so much like condescension because I'd need to remind him of things too. I know some BTs want nothing more than to marry into a family of FFBs, but there are certainly perks to marrying another slightly out-of-sync person.

Last night's dream haunts me while I thread beads onto thick strings before dumping them off, hearing the staccato thunks of them pooling atop one another in the bowl. Sure, we can string them but we can't tie them to make a necklace or a bracelet.

When I look up, it's to meet the eyes of Elan's

mother. I get the feeling she's been studying me for a while. Seated as she is next to Moyshe's wife, I have to wonder if they've been talking about me. Though there's a strict prohibition on gossip, it's probably one of the rules everyone struggles with the most. In this I don't feel so alone.

I smile at her in what I hope is an encouraging, friendly way but she merely narrows her eyes and turns back to her conversation with Shira. And me? I go back to stringing beads, passing the string through the painted wood over and over again until the thread is full, I tip them off, and have to string them on over and over again. Fruitlessly.

BY THE TIME we get home from a boisterous late dinner, Shabbos is over. I know it's supposed to be a day of rest, but I may be even more tired than I was last night after an entire day of forcing a smile onto my face.

Despite my exhaustion and feeling out of sorts, when Elan suggests we go to bed with that hopeful tone in his voice I nod, hoping he doesn't mean merely going to sleep. When he circles fingers around my wrist, tugging me after him, I'm certain. No sleep for us. Not just yet.

Once in the bedroom, he nudges me into a corner, facing me away from where the walls come together.

"Stay there."

I wouldn't have moved anyway, but his terse command ensures it. Trying not to wring my hands, I watch him move about the room. The first thing he does is remove the runner on his side of the bed and fold it neatly before putting it to the side. Then he rummages in the closet and emerges with what looks like a…tarp.

Before I can school my features, my nose wrinkles up. That's alarming. What on earth has he got planned for me? A *tarp*? Luckily he doesn't notice my expression because he's too busy shaking the thing out and spreading it on the floor. A hundred possibilities run through my head, each more disturbing than the last. I try to convince myself that I have a far, far filthier imagination than Elan does, but the man is quite cunning. And dirty.

When the tarp is laid out to his satisfaction, he opens the deep bottom drawer of the nightstand and draws out a few large pillar candles and a box of matches. What is he, setting up mood lighting for whatever it is exactly he's going to do with the tarp?

I don't have more time to wonder, because he turns on me. "Strip. Everything but your tichels."

I expect him to go about his business. Most of the time he undresses me himself but when he orders me to do it, he doesn't watch. But he is now, his gaze so intense I feel like I'm already naked. I move slowly, unbuttoning the sleeveless blouse I'd put on over my shirt, a piece of my old wardrobe I'd been able to salvage. I'd worn it today as some sort of silent protest I'm sure didn't register with anyone else. My face is getting hot under his scrutiny and I swallow, my fingers fumbling at the buttons.

"Don't be nervous, little bird. Not yet. I've been inside you. I've tasted you. What's a little nudity?"

He's right but it doesn't make me feel any better.

When I've removed every last article of my clothing, he orders me to kneel in the center of the tarp. The candles that he's set out on a ceramic plate are right in front of me and he takes the opportunity to light them, knowing my eyes are glued to where he's setting the flames.

When the wicks are alight, the flames glow in the darkened room, their subtle flickering hypnotic. It makes me slightly less self-conscious, but no less confused. Why did he leave me my headscarves? He loves my hair. Loves to close a fist in it and pull, loves to bind it in his ropes. Loves that it's for him and only him. So why is it still bound up in the elaborate thing I styled hoping to impress his family? Which was silly, given that all the women wear sheitels. Like most of the women here.

The smell of the blown out matches permeates the room, smoke curling up to the ceiling. I watch it rise and dissipate, distracting myself from the unknown until his voice startles me.

"On your stomach."

I do as I'm told, stretching out on the tarp and laying my hands alongside my head. My hipbones dig into the wood and my breasts are pressed into the hard floor, but it's not entirely uncomfortable.

When he breaks out several lengths of forest green rope from another drawer of the nightstand, I'm even more at ease. This is familiar. I breathe and watch as he rigs cuffs around my wrists, attaching me to a leg of the bed on one side and a foot of the bureau on the other. I like when he makes me into a work of art with all the intricate knots and weaving of the cords, but there's something sexy too about this workmanlike proficiency. Competence is hot. The only thing I don't like is that it's quickly over and I can't ogle him and his dexterity as he wraps more cuffs around my ankles and affixes those to the remaining posts.

Once I'm in his ropes I don't care so much what else he has in mind. He might hurt me, yes—I'll probably enjoy that part—but he won't harm me. I believe he will honor his promises. Perhaps he'll never be romantic or terribly emotionally intimate with me but he does care and he wouldn't betray my trust. Especially not when I've handed myself over so fully.

He tugs at the ropes, more I think to give me that little thrill of being controlled and contained than to actually check his work, and then he goes once again into the drawer, extracting a blindfold. I lift my head without having to be asked and he fastens the fabric snug around my eyes.

After it's been tied tight, he lays a hand on the back of my neck. "I'll be back in a minute."

I don't respond because he hasn't asked me a question, but when he tightens his grip and shakes me gently, the words come to my lips: "Yes, master."

"You're a little spacey already, aren't you?"

"Yes, master."

There's an unintelligible grunt, but it's accompanied by a stroking of the nape of my neck and then he's gone.

He comes in and out of the room several times. I suppose I should be trying to decipher what all the sounds mean, but he was right. I'm well on my way to subspace and I can't bring myself to care. Besides, it's more fun when it feels like he's doing magic. Why do I want to pull the curtain back? I don't. I just want to enjoy the show, especially after the stress of the day.

Minutes later, his voice rumbles across my consciousness. "Still with me?"

"Yes, master." Even I can hear how dreamy and singsong my voice is. His laugh is tinged with wickedness and I smile in response.

That's when the burning starts.

I yelp and pull at my ropes, panicked by the sensation, but it's only a drop over one of my shoulder blades that quickly becomes tolerable. Followed by another at the base of my spine and another. It all falls into place. The candles, the tarp, why he didn't want me to take down my hair. He's dripping hot wax onto my back. And now that I'm expecting it, though I don't know where the next drop is going to fall, I can control myself more. Well, a little more.

A drop lands just below my armpit and makes a scorching trail down the side of my ribs. I hiss through my teeth. "Fuck."

"Language, Tzipporah," he admonishes in that warning tone that makes me crazy. I swallow to keep the next curse from coming out of my mouth when there's another drip just below the last one. Sadistic fiend.

At last I've had more time to get used to the sensation and I'm not so shocked every time a drop lands. I've found my breathing and it helps me through the splashes searing into my skin. I can tolerate it on my back, but when a drop falls on my upper arm, I squeak and pull at my bonds, rattled. "Master, please, no."

There's a pause and then a movement before his heavy hand is at my neck and his beard is gently rasping behind my ear. "No, what?"

"Not on my arms, please, master. I can take it on my back, but on my arm it hurts so much more."

"And not the good kind?" His voice is gentle and teasing which makes it all the harder to say no.

"No, master. I could—I could take it. If you needed me to, but I—" My chest seizes up with fear at the memory. Not of the pain precisely, because that's near impossible to remember, but with that animal instinct of *run*. It's possible that on some other day, at some other time, I'd be more willing to at least try, but after this nerve-racking Shabbos, it's too much.

He hushes me, rubbing a thumb across my cheek. "Not today. You've been very brave."

Gratification feathers around my heart. I've pleased him. And the "Not today" pleases me. Not that I'll be looking forward to it precisely, because it hurt. A lot. But perhaps he understands that my refusal is due mostly to the circumstances. At least he believes I'm strong enough to take more, and his faith in me in this one small thing heartens me. He soothes me and pets me until I'm settled back into languor and I memorize his touch, what it feels like on my skin and over the wax.

"You can take a little more, though, I think."

"Yes, master," I agree, because I want to. I want to thank him for giving this to me, for showing me what I'm capable of so I will give him this gift.

He stands and I brace myself for the scorching drops falling on my skin and there it is. That blistering heat. I whimper because I've grown unused to it but I sink into the experience more quickly this time. He begins longer pours—not just small drops, but lingering ribbons of wax drizzled over my skin. Everything leaves my head besides sensation: the enduring heat, how the wax feels different when it's poured over covered spots versus untouched skin, the contrast of the cool and crinkly tarp under my cheek.

I am free.

He pours two crescents of wax over my shoulder blades where wings might be. I can almost feel them sprout from my back so I can soar though I'm anchored to the ground. Then he's unfastening the ropes he's tied me with and I feel like I might fly away until he rolls me to my back and pulls the blindfold from my face.

His dark eyes are alive with desire for me. If I'm a bird, he's a hawk and he's going to snatch me right out of the sky. I want to be caught. But first he reaches for the clasp holding my headscarves in place. His fingers are deft, having learned how to unfurl my creations, and it's not long before my hair is loose underneath me, spread out over the tarp.

"Beautiful," he says. "And so good."

He kisses me, his lips and tongue demanding and I

give in to him, letting my legs fall open where he's pressed against me. While our mouths play, he handles my breasts roughly, squeezing and kneading, tweaking and pinching my nipples. It's not long before I'm writhing underneath him and making small, pleading noises between desperate kisses.

"Please. Please, master. I need you. Please."

He torments me for a few more minutes. I've picked up on this little trick of his. Waiting long enough after my requests to make it clear he'll do as he pleases. It's his choice, but part of the calculus is what I want. The effort he puts into the equation melts me.

He strips his clothes, not folding them neatly like he usually does but leaving them in a heap on the bed, and the small detail makes me feel powerful in my own fragile way. Then he's pressing inside of me, no fingers to check if I'm ready because he knows I am. With each forceful thrust, the wax on my back rubs against the tarp, some of it shedding. It creates this unique friction, like nothing I've ever felt before. So many new things he's shown me and there's so much more to see. I take advantage of my hands being free to hold onto him while we're joined, my fingertips digging into the musculature of his back. Not to hurt him—not that I could— but to clasp him to me, to feel as much that he belongs to me as I belong to him.

I feel blessed when we do this, as though we're fulfilling our purpose. It's as if we are one soul.

It doesn't take long before my climax is building. I rock my hips up to get the contact that's going to send me over the edge and he threads fingers through strands of my hair, anchoring my head to the ground, the tension in my scalp sending an extra quiver of lust through me.

"Fly for me, little bird."

His demand sends a gust of wind under me and I spread my wings and glide on it, calling out his name and clutching at him as I come apart. The contractions of my muscles around him encourage his own release and he lets himself go, plunging hard into me as he comes.

When our breath has evened out, he kisses my cheek and nuzzles at me, the unexpectedly fond gesture making me ache. Not that he's unkind otherwise, but I wouldn't mind some affection outside of when we've been intimate. I'll take what I can get though, bask in the warmth of the aftercare and pretend it's more than circumstance, kink, and sex that've drawn us together.

Withdrawing, he offers me a cloth and turns me onto my stomach. I'd forgotten all about the wax, scattered as I am, but the removal certainly reminds me. It doesn't hurt precisely, but there's a tugging, pulling, stripping away that makes me feel like I'm losing a layer of skin. It makes me feel vulnerable in a way I haven't before and tears pool in my eyes before rolling down my face, dripping into my hair and onto my arm where my head is cradled.

It doesn't take Elan long to notice and when he does, he talks to me in low nonsense words, interspersing the removal of the wax with featherlight caresses that feel electric on my sensitized skin. By the end, I'm sobbing and shaking, my entire body on fire like an exposed nerve. But he covers me, comforts me, takes me into his arms and carries me to our small bathroom. Holds me while the bath fills part way and then wedges his huge body into the undersized tub to hold me in the tepid water.

Curled up in his lap, my head resting against his chest, I start to calm. By the time he's helping me dress then spooning me on my side of the bed, he's eased me enough to fall asleep. When I startle awake in the middle of the night, coming to consciousness with the feeling of freefalling with no wings, he's there. He doesn't usually hold me through the night, probably because it's uncomfortable lying on the gap between the beds, but tonight he is. The selfless gesture of concern is touching.

"Go to sleep, little bird. I'm not going anywhere."

I HAVEN'T RETURNED to my habit of retreating to my office in the evenings. I don't crave Elan's company in quite the same way when I'm not niddah, but I figure it's a good precedent to establish. The softer emotional and verbal connections don't seem so important when we're able to come together physically, but my period is getting closer, I can feel it. I'm especially conscious of wanting to build the familiarity now so I have something to hang onto during those twelve days. Not like last time when I was left drowning in loneliness, my wings sodden, no flight possible.

Not to mention that our after-dinner study sessions

have become, secretly, one of my favorite times of the day. Me with my notebooks and papers to grade, Elan on the other side of the table with his Torah or gemora or one of his seforim, his brow wrinkled thoughtfully as he faithfully performs his learning.

I'm in awe of his devotion to his studies. Unlike me, he's not held responsible by a class full of expectant students, and I doubt even Moyshe would comment if he took a night or two off every week.

But no. Nearly every night, unless there's something he needs to attend to for the shop or he's just so bone-tired from a long day that he heads straight to bed after dinner, always he's at our table with his books before we go to sleep. Am I allowed to call his dedication sexy? Because it totally is.

He barely looks up as I put my things down across the table from him but I think there's a vague curl of the corner of his mouth as I sit. The quiet togetherness feels familiar, a casual marker of pleasant domesticity. I'm not sure if he feels that way or if he wishes his strange wife would take her scribbling and annoying habit of reading things I need to clarify out loud to a different room of the apartment. But he's never asked so here I'll sit.

I crack the binder that has my lesson plan in it and look at what's scheduled for my section of the department's intro class the next day. Food, another one of my favorite lectures. I've made it a habit to stop by a kosher bakery on the way to this class because if there's one thing I'm sure of in this life, it's that college students love free food. In the spring I try to schedule this particular lecture near Purim so I can bring hamantaschen. Mostly because aside from brisket, it's my very favorite Jewish food. My fall semester students usually get fallback cookies—rugelach or macaroons.

It's not just about sweets though. One of the reasons I like this lecture is because everyone eats. Everyone understands the notion of dietary restrictions. Though some of my students will no doubt wrinkle their noses because the idea of not being able to eat something "because G-d says so" is far more bizarre to them than because of allergies, or it's not paleo or whatever the latest fad diet is, they're usually quite animated.

While I'm reviewing the strictures of Jain vegetarianism, I have an idea.

"Elan?"

I've clearly called him out of some sort of deep concentration because it takes him a few blinks to focus on me and he looks a little startled.

"I'm sorry, go back to your—"

"It's fine. What do you need?"

Need is a strong word but now that I've interrupted him I can at least ask, not make the disturbance for naught.

"Would you maybe be willing to…" I moisten my lips between my teeth because this is a far bigger ask than I'd thought at first. He'll have to take the time off, he's not overly fond of public speaking, he—

"Tzipporah, what is it? What do you need?"

"Would you come to my afternoon class tomorrow? We're talking about food."

His brows draw together and lines form on his forehead. "You want me to talk to your students?"

"Yes." Now that I've had a minute to think about it, I'm getting even more excited. "They'll love you."

Suspicion turns his head and he eyes me warily. "Why? Because they've never seen an Orthodox Jewish man before? They want a matched set?"

Why is that the first place his mind goes? Something unflattering? Granted, my first-year survey students aren't always the most sensitive and I've had to cultivate patience in dealing with some of their less couth questions, but they're generally on their best behavior with visitors.

"No. They get bored listening to me yammer on and on day in and day out. They like guest speakers. And you know you're far more proficient with Jewish dietary restrictions than I am."

The last is a bit of a joke. I can poke fun at myself now because I feel as though he's not so disappointed when I absent-mindedly mess up keeping kosher anymore. He's accepted it as a price of being married to me, one I hope he doesn't find too high. Dare I hope he's even come to find it close-to-if-not-quite endearing? It hadn't been so insulting when he shook his head when I'd confessed my latest kitchen transgression.

"All right, my little bird," he'd said after I'd accidentally grabbed a milk ladle and stirred the boiling-over chicken soup with it. "I was in the mood for shawarma anyhow. But next time, pay more attention, yes?"

I'd nodded, and as we'd put on light coats to protect

against the crisp late fall air, he'd kissed me on the forehead and I'd flushed with delight. But now he doesn't seem to find it funny.

"I don't think so. Not this time." He's tried to soften the blow by hinting he might be game in the future, but I feel his refusal acutely.

"Of course. You'd probably need to give Reuven more notice than that." Yes, I'll make his excuses for him, to myself. Then maybe this won't feel so bad.

IN THE MORNING, I stop by the bakery on my way to the subway and get one package of rugelach. Then think better of it and pick out a box of macaroons as well. And then think still better and grab two of each. College students are like human garbage disposals.

Arriving at my classroom with my sack of goodies, I've managed to shrug off the touchy mood I've found myself in since last night. It really is fine that Elan didn't want to come today. As Bina was perceptive enough to point out, he doesn't have a great fondness for words. And while it's one thing to stand up in front of a community you've been a part of for your entire life and talk on a subject you've studied for almost as long, it's another entirely to be thrust in front of a roomful of strangers, some of whom, as much as I'd like to deny it, will likely do some amount of pointing and staring.

Strangely, though I feel like he could vanquish any foe, I think my towering husband might be shy, like an elephant afraid of a mouse. Maybe in the spring if I give him more warning and he has some time to get used to the idea and prepare, he'll agree.

My students devour the cookies as I knew they would, although they seem to prefer the rugelach to the macaroons, a partiality I make note of for next year. Halfway through the lecture, Scott, who continues to sit in the back, raises his hand.

"Where did you get these?" His question is barely intelligible due to his mouth being stuffed full but I can just make out the words.

"I'll tell you in just a minute. Let's finish talking about fish Fridays, shall we?"

When we've covered the Catholic tradition of not eating meat on Fridays, I turn to my own dietary observances. Keeping kosher is complicated but I try to simplify as well as I can without glossing over important elements. I tell them about the bakery and about Elan's shop. How busy they are on Thursday afternoons and Friday mornings, how it's been in the family for generations. I tell them about my own difficulties observing kashrut, which they laugh about, knowing by this point in the semester that yes, I can be a bit scatterbrained.

And though he's not there, I can picture Elan in the back row of my class, rolling his eyes indulgently when I relate the brisket incident. Perhaps when I tell him about it over dinner, he'll have regained his sense of humor enough to be entertained.

CHAPTER SEVEN

AFTER MY LATE seminar on Thursday, I make my way home. It's nearing darkness and the streets in my neighborhood are mostly empty because people are inside their homes, having dinner with their families. Which is where I'm supposed to be.

I can't help but enjoy the nights that Elan cooks. Not that he's got a fantastic track record—the curry's been the definitive winner—but there's a weight taken off of me because it's one night I don't have to worry that I'll screw something up in the kitchen and we'll have to kasher something or worse yet throw something out...again. He also tends to feel quite proud of himself. Not only has he brought home the metaphorical bacon, but he's also fried it up in the pan. I think he enjoys the idea of providing for me even though we keep our finances mostly separate.

And that good, I-Am-Man mood usually translates to the bedroom. Which I certainly appreciate, oh yes I do. He treats me like a ragdoll and I can't get enough. The thought is enough to put more of a spring in my step.

I bounce up the stairs, eager not so much to eat the food he's cooked, but to see his expression when he shows it to me.

"Elan?"

There's no banging of pots and pans or muttered Yiddish curses coming from the kitchen so perhaps he's done already? But when I come into the dining room, he's seated at the table, slump-shouldered and with no dinner on the table.

For a moment, I feel a small and guilty rush. Did he screw up keeping kosher? Not that I'd be happy about that precisely—and it would be one mistake he's made to my several—but it would make me feel less silly. Except I don't think he'd look quite so crestfallen and weary if that were the case.

"What's wrong?"

His brows gather and he takes a deep breath. Has someone died? Because he may be moody, but never sad. Not so defeated.

"A few of your students came to my shop today."

"They did?"

"Yes."

It's surprising that any of the predominantly waspy kids in my classes would venture into this neighborhood, but that doesn't explain why he's so upset.

His face grows more distorted in thought and the movement of his beard telegraphs the clench of his jaw before he spreads his hands on the table.

"I know I haven't been perfect, but I've tried to be a

good husband to you. I've provided the things I'm supposed to, fulfilled my obligations. And I know things haven't always been easy for you here, but I thought you were happy. I thought this was the life you wanted."

"You have been a good husband." Not precisely ideal, to be so close to everything I've ever wanted and yet so far…but good. Definitely good. Everyone should be so lucky as to have a spouse like Elan. I won't lie and say that I'm happy, though, because his perfection in so many areas highlights the decided lack of love. "And this is the life I want. I've found the way I'm meant to honor Hashem. I don't feel as if I'm searching anymore."

"Then why did your students show up to my store, the girls wearing short skirts and camisoles it was far too cold for? Why were the boys pointing at the women you call your friends and saying unkind things about them? Like how they're brainwashed and subservient? And why, Tzipporah, did they think it was so funny to come up to my counter and ask for pork and ham and bacon?"

The image of Elan standing at his place of business that has been in his family for so long, hands curling into fists on the steel surface as he tried so very hard not to lose his temper while these ignorant kids goaded him, it breaks my heart. And makes me furious. For him, but also for my community. And for myself.

I shared my life with my students hoping to make the subject matter more relatable, entertaining. Never did I dream they would take something I'd said and turn it into something so ugly. It makes me sick to my stomach. I'll have to think about how to address this, but in the meantime I owe my husband an apology.

"I'm so sorry."

"If you're unhappy, I wish you would have asked me for a divorce. I'll give you one and you can go back to your old life. Maybe you'll be happier there."

"Why would I want that? I didn't send them there, if that's what you think. I would never—"

He waves a hand and the movement seems to sap him of even more strength. "I don't think that. You wouldn't do something that cruel. But maybe you've said things. Like how we're strange and foreign and we have all these ridiculous rules. I've defended you to people here, the ones who said you'd leave, the ones who said you wouldn't make a good wife. Even before that. I've said I thought your intentions were pure of heart even if you get it wrong sometimes, which is harder to find than any rote performance of mitzvot. But perhaps I was wrong. Perhaps we're just another one of your studies."

That's so unfair and not true at all. Yes, I've thought idly about ending our marriage, but never, until I was absolutely sure we couldn't work it out would I say it out loud. But to know he's stood up for me, just not in my hearing, provides a warm note to the cold flooding my veins. "Elan—"

The screech of the chair as he pushes it behind him cuts me off and when he's standing there so big and so obviously trying to contain his anger, it's hard to find my words. I don't know that he'd be able to hear me through the shroud of dejection hanging over him anyway.

"I'm going to Moyshe's house." Of course, his incredibly rigid brother who hasn't warmed to me at all. "I'll be back later tonight. There's dinner in the fridge for you."

THOUGH I HEAR Elan come in sometime in the middle of the night, I don't say anything. I don't know what else to say because I'm beyond humiliated and hurt and I can imagine his feelings are exponential. I don't think I'll ever sleep, but apparently I manage at least a few hours because when I wake in the morning, Elan is gone. Without a word. Without a note. It's not unusual for him to leave for morning services at the shul before I get up but it feels bad somehow.

I ghostwalk through making a kugel to bring to Bina's later, my head occupied with what Elan said. Do I treat my home and my family like some community to be observed and deconstructed? A collection of pieces and parts to be poked at and analyzed? When doing my research, I do my best to be respectful of the norms of the community without sacrificing my own beliefs and I always urge my students to do the same.

Yes, I've put my skills as a researcher to use in Forest Park, although not consciously most of the time. They're just part of me: the way I think, the way I learn, a lens through which I see the world. But I don't think I put on my scholar hat when I come home at the end of the day. If anything, I feel as though I take off all my hats—

advisor, teacher, researcher—when I'm here and what I'm left with are my headscarves, my commitment to my faith, the deepest and truest part of me.

After depositing the kugel in the fridge, I manage to stumble my way to the subway, across the crowded campus, and into my classroom. Luckily the class I'm teaching today is a topic I've taught a thousand times before, something I probably talk about in my sleep: the role of language in religion. And though the students seem somewhat less engaged than in past years, I suspect it has more to do with me than them. I feel like a zombie.

I end class a little early and clear my throat. "I wanted to take a minute to speak with you all. It has come to my attention that a few of my students visited my husband's place of business yesterday and were not very respectful of him or of our community." *Our, Elan. I said our, because I mean it. I do.* "I'm not sure if it was students from this class or one of my other sections, but I wanted to say—"

What do I want to say? I look out at the rows of students, many slumped behind their fold-down desks, pens dangling from fingers, but all eyes are riveted on me.

"I know the way I dress and some of the traditions I keep seem strange to many of you. I wasn't raised as an Orthodox Jew, so to be honest, some of them seem strange to me too. But this is the life I have chosen to lead. No one has coerced me into it, and though I've made more mistakes than I can count, on the whole, they have accepted me and supported me. Even if they hadn't, they don't deserve to be treated like animals in a zoo."

The image of my students pointing at Bina or any of the other women who have befriended me, and saying cruel things about them wrings out my heart. And how could they possibly say those things when I come here day after day and perform my job admirably? I'm a good professor, maybe the best lecturer in the department, and my research has been well-received. Not to mention that in my personal life, I left a man and a life I didn't find satisfying and found another. Brainwashed and subservient my butt.

There's a tightness around my throat that I want to clear, but if I do, I might cry. That's best avoided. Because heaven forfend someone in academia have feelings about *anything*, never mind being violated in this very personal way. I also realize as I say the words that it's true. The people who have been unkind or suspicious of me are a small minority now. I have proven myself and I have been accepted. I should try to let go of the rest, even if they happen to be my in-laws.

And Elan…he's never done anything to deserve this. His only fault was marrying me and I hate the fact that I've caused him nothing but pain and embarrassment. We can end this ill-advised marriage if he wishes to and he can find a wife better suited to him. In the meantime, I won't allow anyone to disparage or ridicule him.

"My husband is a good man. He is kind and hardworking and he does not deserve your mockery. Please leave him and my community out of this. If you have questions about my faith, you may come to me directly and I'll be happy to speak with you. Class is dismissed."

My students are usually rowdy as they leave because our session is the last thing standing between them and the weekend, but today there's a definite pause before anyone heads for the door. And when they do, it's in a herd of whispers and shuffles.

I pack up my notes and other things, conscious as ever of the time. The days are Autumn-long, but I can't dally if I want to make it all the way to my stop before I have to get off the subway, never mind light the candles. I must be more focused (or perhaps less?) than I thought because when I turn to the exit, two of my students are waiting for me. Stephanie and Mike.

"Professor Klein, we wanted to say—"

"I actually don't have time for this. I need to get home before Shabbos starts. If you have something you'd like to discuss, you're welcome to come by during my office hours next week or make an appointment. Excuse me."

A remorseful glance passes between them but they trail out of the small auditorium, muttering something to each other. I think I've found some of the culprits. And next week, if they don't come to me themselves, I'll be asking them to stay after class. I won't report their atrocious behavior to the university, but I need to do something about it. Best thought of when I'm not rigid with anger and I want to yell.

I get the rest of my things packed up and ready to go. This week's Shabbos may very well be even more uncomfortable than last's. At least I'd felt as though Elan was on my side whereas now the only friendly face will be Bina's. I'll just have to glue myself to her side, there's nothing else for it.

Before I can head out the door though, someone calls to me from halfway up the stairs. "Tzipporah."

My emotional turmoil must be causing me to hallucinate, because there's no other reason Elan would be standing in my lecture hall in his dark suit and spotless white shirt, his kippah visible from this angle because for once, I'm standing above him.

"Why are you here?"

"I came here to give you a divorce."

My heart falls into my stomach. I knew he was upset but I didn't think it was this bad. He hasn't even given me a chance to explain.

"Elan, please. Don't do this. Give me a chance. I—" And then my sorrow transmutes into anger. This is incredibly unfair. I'm being punished for the actions of others and he's being so unreasonable that it makes me want to scream. I have tried to be what he wants, and to be written off so quickly as a mistake sets off a flurry of objections. "What do I have to do to pass muster? When will you stop doubting me? I just want you to love me. I know I'm not Rivka, your perfect Jewish wife, but I'm doing the best I can. Rabbi Horowitz and Bina think I'm good enough. When will I be good enough for you? You're the one whose opinion I value the most."

The very thing I was most afraid of not being able to have is the very thing I've been handed. But it's not enough. Apparently while I was praying, I forgot to ask for someone who would love me. Who would look at me adoringly and not just with lust-glazed eyes. Thinking it would be enough was so very foolish of me.

"I don't want to love you, Tzipporah."

People who say words can't hurt you are idiots. None of Brooks' mocking, none of the tortures Elan's visited upon my body, none of the blatantly disparaging looks I get have ever hurt me so much as those small words. *I don't want to love you.* I open my mouth to say something, but no words come out. He's stolen them.

"I have spent my entire adult life defending myself and my choices to my family. Even before she got sick, Rivka couldn't have children. Did you know that?"

"No. I'm sorry."

"There's nothing to be sorry about. I mourned, of course, because we both wanted to have a family. I would've been happy to adopt but she was set on the idea of experiencing pregnancy and childbirth. It took her a long time to even admit we might need help. We argued about it a lot, but I still loved her. Very much."

I know he did. It's on his face every time he talks about her. The reverence and affection painful reminders of things he withholds from me.

"My parents though, they wanted grandchildren and they wanted me to leave her. *Find a proper Jewish wife*, they said, *one who will give you children, no matter how.* I fought them every day. It got better when Moyshe and Dovid got married and started families but it got worse when Rivka got sick. They couldn't wait for her to die."

Restrained rage makes his voice hoarse. I can only imagine how hard that must have been for him, fighting to keep Rivka alive or at the very least comfortable, all the while his parents wishing for her death. What monsters.

"They didn't say that of course but I could tell what they were thinking…" Of course not. Because wishing for someone's death is not a very Jewish attitude to hold. The sanctity of life is everything; almost all other laws can be cast aside if it means a life can be saved. So no they'd never admit that, but I'm sure he felt it.

He shakes his head and I want to hold him. Comfort him. No one should have so much asked of them, not even this man who could carry the world on his back and not break a sweat. But he has been carrying it and it's so very heavy. "It wasn't so long before my mother started urging me to get married again. I resisted even after I was ready out of stubbornness, and when Bina offered you…to be honest, part of the attraction was that I knew they wouldn't want me to choose you. *She's too committed to her job, Elan. Too set in her ways. Choose someone who's not so…strange. Someone younger, more likely to give you children. Does she even want babies?*"

The listing of my faults makes me clutch at my arms folded across my chest, my fingertips probably leaving bruises. Some of it is nonsense and I know it—I'd love to fill our house with children and I've already changed how I live my life drastically in my attempts to adhere to my faith. But some of it is true and there's nothing I can do about it. I can't be younger, and I've tried to fit in here but I'll always be a bird trying to swim in the ocean, having to come up for air periodically because otherwise I'll drown. Foolish.

"So you don't love me." I can bear that, right? Brooks didn't love me, nor was he particularly kind. He didn't respect my faith or my need for pain and domination. Elan gives me all of those things. He respects me, values me, fulfills my needs in the bedroom. I should be grateful instead of feeling like my bones are uncomfortably hollow. Or...I can leave. As he's come here to tell me to do.

"I didn't say that."

My eyes snap to his, his tense jaw, his knitted brows.

"But you—"

"You're usually so good at listening, Tzipporah."

I rewind our conversation back in my mind but it seems so clear. I'm not the wife he wants and he doesn't feel like bearing the responsibility of defending me and my myriad quirks to all and sundry. I'm a burden to him and he's borne enough for one lifetime. I can't say I blame him but it hurts.

"I said I didn't *want* to love you. I didn't say I *didn't* love you."

He lets the words hang in the air, drifting slowly to the floor.

"I have a confession to make." His lips purse guiltily and he looks away. What has he done? "I followed you here today. Though I hoped you wouldn't, I half-expected you to leave the house and dig a backpack out of a bush along the way. Change into pants and a short-sleeve shirt. I didn't want to believe that our life was a joke to you, but after your students came into my shop…"

I can see how that might fan the flames of his doubt, particularly if his family's been adding kindle to it.

"Did you know there's a little alcove just over there?" He tips his head toward the front of the lecture hall where he's come from. "It's cramped but it can fit a man."

I know the alcove he's talking about. I refrain from telling him I've stumbled upon a pair of students having a, uh, rendezvous there when I had to retrieve some notes I forgot. He'd be horrified.

"I took the subway, I walked the campus. And I realized how strong your faith is. I have it easy, being surrounded by people who look like me, talk like me. Even the ones who don't are familiar with the mores of the neighborhood. No one blinks an eye at my tzitzit, my kippah. But every day, you wear your modest clothes and your beautiful tichels and you go out in the world. I saw people stare at you, I heard a few of them talk and you must too. It can't be easy but you do it. It fills me with pride that my wife is so devout. I thought so before but now I've seen it. And to hear you teach your class, impart your wisdom to your students with humor and compassion. It filled my heart so full I thought it might burst."

He clutches his chest as if it hurts, as if he's feeling the ache anew and I feel an answering throb behind my breast bone. To hear him say these things is exhilarating.

"I've been trying to convince myself that what I felt for you was some mash of duty and defiance and animal attraction. It's not. Sometimes my love for you is so big I feel that I'm drowning in it. It's a fearsome thing, to be tasked with caring for a woman like you. So intelligent, so vibrant. I pray every night to be worthy but in the daylight, it feels dangerous to love you so much. It's easier to be quiet when my family criticizes you. To shrug and let them believe I've made a mistake and that staying with you is the honorable thing to do. It's not. It's selfish and I owe you more than that."

I have to scrub at my eyes because I don't want to mar this moment with tears but I can barely contain myself. He loves me?

"From now on I won't allow them to speak of you like that ever. Not in my presence. And I promise to give myself to you as you've always given yourself to me. Completely. Please have faith in me in this as you have faith in me in everything else. Tzipporah, I love you."

Before I can leave any room for a sliver of doubt, I fly down the stairs and into his arms. He catches me up as if I weigh nothing and holds me against his body, my feet off the ground. "I love you too, Elan. I've just been afraid. That you didn't think I was good enough. That I didn't please you and—"

"You do, little bird. You do. I promise you that. Even when you make mistakes, I love you and I'm so proud you're mine."

He puts me down and cradles my face in his hands, brushing away the few tears that have managed to escape through my lashes. Tears finally of happiness.

"Now let's get home so we can observe Shabbos properly. I know how important that is to you."

"It is," I sniff and he grins. "Besides, the kugel I made is perfection."

"I don't doubt it. Not one bit."

EPILOGUE

One Year Later

"**T**URN."

I spin half way around, leaving my arms out so he can see his handiwork. He hooks a finger under a strand of rope and pries it looser, evening out the tension. I don't know how he does it, but he always seems to know just where these things need to be adjusted.

He looks awfully pleased with himself and I can't wait to look at his creation in the mirror. It feels good, certainly. A web of rope around my chest, holding me and reminding me that he's with me even when we're far apart. He used a vibrant turquoise today, one that complements my hair. Both of them secrets I share only with him.

"Go look," he says, knowing I'm practically bouncing on my toes with impatience. I want to see too. I flit over to the closet and open it to reveal the full-length mirror on the other side of the door.

"Oh." I could tell when he was weaving it that the harness he tied around my chest was more intricate than usual. Sometimes it's just a hastily tied cuff above my elbow, or a single strand belted around my waist. Though it hasn't been an issue for months, when I'd been niddah he'd leave a bracelet for me on my dresser since he couldn't touch me to tie something on, but always I have his rope on me when I leave the house.

I knew today's project was on the fancier end of the spectrum, but I hadn't expected this. He's somehow managed to fashion the knots and the strands to look like abstract wings. It's utterly beautiful and it brings tears to my eyes. Not just the product, but the time and thought and effort that went into creating this for me. *I am my beloved's and my beloved is mine.* Of course it doesn't help that I'm more emotional these days.

He steps closer until his body is pressed the length of mine, his front against my back as his arms come around me and his big hands cup my swelling belly. He has something to hold onto now, with me being seven months pregnant, but even before I'd started to show, he'd done this and it delights me.

"Do you like it?"

"It's beautiful, Elan. Thank you."

I know well enough by now that his gruff noise is actually thinly masked joy. My opinion of him matters so much to him, as much as his opinion matters to me. I do my best to let him know in words how much I appreciate everything he does for me, how much I want him and need him, though it embarrasses him sometimes.

He kisses the side of my neck and I tilt my head in invitation. He nibbles and sucks at the sensitive skin for delectable minutes until I've been reduced to a puddle, but he stops suddenly and swats at my behind.

"No time for that, you temptress. I don't want you late for school."

Yes, right, school. I'm finishing out the semester, but then the baby will arrive and I'm taking a leave of absence. We've let his parents think it's permanent and mine believe it's temporary. In truth, we're undecided. We'll figure it out.

My pregnancy has eased things with our families some. My parents are excited to add to their small brood of grandchildren and are crossing their fingers for a boy since they have only granddaughters so far, but I don't think they really care either way. They've also stayed over for Shabbos once. They seemed bemused by it all—the services, the rituals, the restrictions—but they tried and that's what matters the most.

Elan's mother clucks over me constantly and my sisters-in-law have been friendlier as well. Everyone loves to talk about babies. I'm sure there's more conflict to come and I'm not entirely comfortable that it took getting pregnant for them to warm to me, but hopefully over time they'll value me for more than giving Elan a child. In the meantime, I'll bask in his love for me.

He helps me dress and watches as I bind up my hair. When I'm presentable, he walks me to the subway stop, his face delightfully covetous as he bids me a simple goodbye. What he's not saying is that he'll be thinking about me all day, planning what to do with me tonight, how best to launch his little bird into the sky. He's given me the gift of flight and a safe place to land when my wings grow tired. My life, my love, my Elan.

Glossary

Please note that these are **very simplified definitions for the purpose of this novella**

Ba'alat Teshuva/BT: a person who was born Jewish but was not raised as observant who later becomes observant

Chavrusa: religious study in which a pair of students analyze and discuss a shared text

Chossen: groom

Dvar Torah: a talk or essay on a portion of the Torah

Frum: religious, observant, sometimes used in place of the word Orthodox

Gemora: a component of the Talmud (a religious text)

Hashem: literally The Name, an alternate way observant Jews refer to G-d

Kallah: bride

Kasher: to render kosher

Kashrut: the body of Jewish laws pertaining to dietary laws

Kippah: yarmulke

Mezuzah: a parchment (frequently contained in a decorative case) inscribed with religious texts and attached to doorposts in a Jewish home

Mikveh: a bath used for ritual immersion in Judaism

Mitzvot: the collection of commandments observant Jews adhere to

Niddah: a term for a woman who is menstruating or who hasn't completed immersion in the mikveh after the end of her period

Rebbetzin: wife of a rabbi

Seforim: religious books

Seminary: post-high school institution of religious education for women (men would study at a yeshiva)

Shabbos: the Jewish Sabbath

Sheitel: a wig worn by some married Orthodox Jewish women in compliance with the code of modesty

Shiva: a period of formal mourning for the dead

Shul: synagogue

Tichel: a headscarf worn by some married Orthodox Jewish women in compliance with the code of modesty

Torah: Jewish law, the first five books of the Bible

Tzitzit: fringes or tassels worn by Jewish men as a reminder of commandments

Yeshiva: an Orthodox Jewish college

Yichud: the room in which a husband and wife spend their first moment alone together

Acknowledgements

I want to thank AJ and Teresa for their always helpful and honest feedback, and of course the comments that make me giggle. You're the best CPs a girl could ask for.

A super special thank you to KK for reading several drafts of this story, and for being willing to share her culture and neighborhood with me. Any remaining mistakes or misunderstandings are entirely mine. You have been exceedingly generous with me, and there are no words to express my gratitude. Sweet potato salad and limonana forever!

Another special thank you to Shannon for submitting the original prompt to the Goodreads BDSM group's Bring Out Your Kink writing event. This has been a huge but delightful challenge, and I'm grateful for the inspiration. While I'm at it, thank you to the Goodreads BDSM group for putting together this event.

Gratitude to the usual suspects: irl friends MTS, EH and LG for listening to my overly enthusiastic chatter, my cover designer Amber for once again saving me from myself while making something beautiful, Mr. Parker who only did the slightest head tilt when I told him what I was going to write about, Nicole the Blurb Queen, and my proofreaders Michele and Christine.

And last but in no way least, to my readers and reviewers: thank you for joining me for something a little different. I hope you enjoyed your time with Tzipporah and Elan as much as I did. Without you, I would be writing into the void. I hope you know how much I appreciate you spending your time and energy on my words.

About the Author

Tamsen Parker is a stay-at-home mom by day, erotic romance writer by naptime. She lives with her family outside of Boston, where she tweets too much, sleeps too little, and is always in the middle of a book. She should really start drinking coffee. You can find out more about Tamsen at tamsenparker.com, follow her on Twitter at @TamsenParker or on Pinterest as tamsenparker or friend her on Facebook at www.facebook.com/tamsenparkerauthor.

Other Books by Tamsen

The Compass Series

Personal Geography

Intimate Geography

Uncharted Territory

Single Titles

Craving Flight

Anthologies

Winter Rain

If you enjoyed Elan and Tzipporah, give Cris and India a try. Read on for the first chapter in their story.

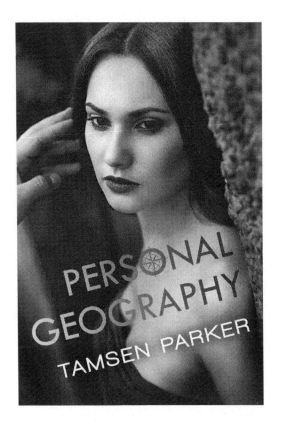

Chapter One

'M SULKING WITH my head in Rey's lap after a dinner of the finest sushi and sake San Diego has to offer.

"Why can't you like women?"

"Same reason you can't. I could give you a good hiding just the same."

A split-second of indecision later, I roll my eyes, wrench my mouth sideways, and sigh. "Don't bother."

"But you're so pretty when you pout, kitten." Rey runs his hands through my hair, kneading talented fingers into my scalp.

"I know." I shrug, purring under his attentions. "But what the hell good does that do me with you?"

"None. Absolutely none. But don't you fear. I'll find you what you crave yet, Scout's honor."

"Were you really a Boy Scout, Rey?" He's not exactly outdoorsy, although very handy with knots.

He scoffs, as I expected. "Have you seen those uniforms? Even six-year-old me was screaming, 'Oh, *hell*, no.'"

I laugh, imagining raven-haired mini-Rey spouting obscenities as his long-suffering mother tried to make him into a joiner: *A neckerchief? What the fuck are you thinking?*

Rey shakes his head. "But back to you. You're not giving me much time."

"It's what I've got. I'm not thrilled about it either, but it's now or not for two months. I don't expect miracles. He doesn't need to be perfect. Just...serviceable."

It's not like I'm looking for Prince Charming. I don't have the time, never mind the inclination, to be searching for *The One*. I just need Rey to find me someone who can dull the sharp edges, slake my thirst to be dominated. At least until the next time.

Rey's handsome copper face settles into pensiveness. It's when he looks like this I call him Professor Walter. *Oh, my beloved Reyes. You would've made a wonderful professor.* But what fun would that be? He's far more suited to his current profession. And I suppose he is a professor of sorts—just not the kind who'll ever get tenure anywhere except in the hearts and minds of his students. Or, as he'd say, clients.

He tries to keep it professional, but for Rey, everything is deeply personal. I've never known someone with such a strong calling. Helping people navigate the wide world of kink is his vocation, and his talent for absolute discretion means he's sought after by some incredibly rich, powerful, private people who want to learn without having to venture into the community to do it. They pay handsomely for his specific services.

I met Rey my freshman year at Princeton, when he was the chipper RA welcoming me to my dorm. He's been more or less mentor, more or less friend ever since. That was ten years ago, and I still remember every single word of our first encounter.

When he'd introduced himself, the too-firm grip of his hand had caught my attention in a way that made my lips part. I'd stuttered when I told him my name.

"I-India Burke. You can call me Indie. Everybody does."

He'd raised a wicked eyebrow, smirked, and hadn't let go of my hand. "That's not a very good reason to be called something, now is it? Because you've always been?"

"I 'spose not," I'd granted, flushing.

"That stops here, little one. So which is it—India or Indie?"

"India," I'd said with certainty and a smile.

His confidence was infectious, and I'd melted at his response: "Well done, little one. Welcome to Princeton, India Burke. The world is now your oyster."

There had been no surprise, only comfort, when he called me "little one"—a total lack of the embarrassment or intimidation I'd always felt around really good-looking men. That's what he was: a man, not a boy. With the way he talked, the way he carried himself, I barely believed he was twenty-two and not thirty-two. He was so sure, so certain. I could feel the poise leaking into my hand from his. Yes, that was my introduction to my beloved Rey, who has made all the difference.

I don't like to think about where I would've ended up without him. He showed me a world I might never had known existed and taught me how to move in it safely and with grace. He keeps me tethered to it with the thinnest of strings, letting me dip a toe in without drowning. I soothe myself by thinking I'll never have to do without. His thighs are lean and muscular under my head as he continues to work his hands over my skull. I sigh with pleasure, about to fall asleep.

"Vasili?"

I wrinkle my nose and open my eyes. "You know I don't like him. I can take a beating as well as anyone—"

"Better, for such a pretty little thing."

I tip my chin in thanks before going on. "But he hit me in the face, and you know how I feel about that."

"I do. I forgot—the fucker. I'm sorry. I won't ask you about him again."

"I forgive you. I know it's hard to keep track. Sometimes I forget." It's quite the long and growing list.

"What about Ethan? You liked him, right?"

"I did, but he's got a girl now and I don't want to share."

"Luke?"

"Meh."

"I think Strider would like to see you again."

"Find me someone who hasn't named himself after a Lord of the Rings character and we'll talk."

Rey snickers. He knows I find it hard to take that guy seriously, which ruins the effect. He might as well have called himself Frodo.

"Takeo?"

"Too fussy. He spends too much time tying me up and not enough time getting me off."

"You're awfully demanding for a submissive, did you know that?" he teases, tugging on my hair.

"Only for you," I promise, batting my eyelashes.

"I know. You're a good little pet otherwise. I rarely hear complaints."

I allow myself to preen under his praise. Damn straight he doesn't hear many complaints. However picky I may be now, I never let my displeasure show when I'm with them. I took that backhand from Vasili like a champ. I only sniffed, letting a single tear roll theatrically down my cheek even as I inwardly seethed that I had to work on Monday and fuck if I was going to answer questions about a black eye.

I probably should've safed out after that, but I was deep in the scene and hadn't wanted to stop. It had been far too long since my last play date, and I was desperate. Besides, the damage was already done. What would a safeword have accomplished except to interrupt the flow? If he'd done it again, I would've called it. Probably. Rey had chastised me afterward for letting it go and made me put it in all my contracts since.

"Let me make some calls, and I'll get back to you. Do you care where?"

"Anywhere but here." I close my eyes under his cossetting.

Rey stays as late as he can, catching the last shuttle

back to San Francisco despite my invitation to stay the night. I don't have a spare bedroom, but it's not unusual for him to sleep in my bed. He's even got drawers—plural—one in the closet and one in the bathroom.

"I've got an early meeting with a prospect, but I'll call you as soon as I've got something."

I wrap my arms tight around him one last time. "I need this."

"I know, little one. I won't let you down." He presses a kiss to the top of my head and hugs me back.

I let him go reluctantly, but I'll see him soon. Probably next week, to debrief about my weekend with DTBD—Dom to Be Determined. This has the same potential it always has: to be a fucking disastrous nightmare or ridiculously hot. It's usually somewhere in the middle. Although with the state I'm in? It would have to be pretty bad for me to score it worse than tepid. The internal spring that coils tight when I'm stressed or uneasy is wound to the breaking point. I need some relief.

I wave my last goodbye as Rey turns the corner and go get ready for bed. I've got an early morning myself, so I only bother with the barest of bedtime routines before I slide between my cool sheets and fall into a restless sleep.

THE NEXT MORNING, Adam kicks my ass.

I bitch as he urges me into another lunge. "Jesus,

Adam, I haven't even had my fucking coffee."

"And now you're not going to need it, are you, princess?"

I give him my best withering glare, the one that makes my assistant quake and my underlings scatter. Adam doesn't blink.

"Come on, you cream puff. Let's get on with it. I haven't got all day," he barks. Bark is accurate. I'm sure lots of girls would fawn over Adam—even in San Diego, he sticks out as a consummate beach body—but to me, he's a friendly mutt. Maybe a golden retriever. Adorable, loyal, and nice to have around, but thoroughly unremarkable.

I roll my eyes and do his bidding for the next half hour before grabbing my bag to head to work. I've made it a habit not to shower at the gym. It might be more convenient, certainly less nasty than plopping myself onto a towel and driving in dripping with sweat, but my club doesn't have private showers and I don't feel like having people stare at me. Not that they would most of the time. I have a nice body, I work hard to keep it that way between my crazy work hours and piles of takeout, but it's nothing extraordinary in this SoCal hell hole. But on occasion, I would get some strange and possibly horrified looks. Do I feel like telling Susie Treadmill that, yes, those are stripes from a cane across my ass? No, I don't. So it's a towel slung over my leather upholstery and a sticky drive to my office where my private bathroom is waiting for me.

WHEN I ARRIVE at quarter to eight, Lucy is already at her desk. "Good morning, Ms. Burke."

It would be rude to respond to her chirping with, "Fuck off, Lucy," right? I wouldn't win Miss Congeniality on my best days, but for the past two weeks, I've been in an especially foul mood. It's been well over a month since my last hook-up, and I'm edgy as fuck. I settle for, "Coffee?"

"Of course, Ms. Burke. And Mr. Valentine asked for you to come to his office as soon as you got in." She takes in my current state, her brown eyes disapproving as always when I come straight from the gym. "But…"

"I'll be there in ten."

"Yes, Ms. Burke."

Her chipper efficiency makes me ill. Even her reddish hair is bobbing cheerfully. If only she were half as good as she sounds. As she looks. She could play a secretary on *Mad Men*. Maybe she should.

I shower and dress, slipping into a grey sleeveless dress and my signature black Louboutins, praying Lucy will have my coffee ready when I walk out my door. But, as always…

"Lucy! Coffee?" I cannot face Jack without it, not when I'm walking into this blind. There are a dozen things he could want to talk to me about, but I'm betting on the LAHA project.

I'm a consultant to public sector agencies. All that waste and bureaucracy people complain about in government? They hire me to clean it up. I get paid to tell people what they're doing wrong and how to fix it—professional bitch, a job built for me. I've dealt with some high-profile projects, ranging from restructuring the Santa Monica mayor's office to administering the public process of a proposed freeway, but LAHA... This is huge.

LAHA is how we refer to the Los Angeles Housing Authority. It's currently in receivership, which is what happens when an agency is so broken they're not allowed to fix themselves and HUD hires a babysitter. In this case, my firm: Jack Valentine Associates. It's a huge coup for us—me especially since Jack's made me his number two on this. It's an enormous undertaking by definition, and while I understood the basic premise of public housing coming into this, the industry is a morass of regulations and the nitpickiest requirements I've ever seen.

I think we're out of our depth, but there's no way in hell Jack would ever admit defeat. Instead, he's been riding everyone twice as hard to make this work. That's meant ninety-hour weeks and piles of takeout. Not to mention an extra and extremely unpleasant new duty for me.

Jack hates press. Abhors how he looks in newspaper photos, detests how he comes across in sound bites, and loathes how red his face gets when someone asks him a hard question he doesn't immediately have an answer to. So now this falls on my shoulders. I'd come as close to begging as I ever have with him to please, please not make me do this. I'm no more thrilled about the idea of being in the public eye than he is, but he was insistent, so here I am—the new public face of JVA.

But I don't think we're talking about press conferences today. No, today we're talking about the report due to HUD on Thursday—or so he bellows at me as soon as I set foot in his office. This is one of the things Jack likes about me: my ability to be yelled at without blinking. It's how he communicates. If you listen hard enough between all the curses, he's telling you what he wants and how he wants it done. But if you're too busy bursting into tears, you're not going to catch that, are you?

I take a seat and scribble notes while he—salt-and-pepper hair already in disarray, blue eyes blazing—rages at top volume. He's taken his suit coat off, his tie's been flung over a standing lamp, and he's pacing while he shouts. It's a good thing Lucy got her shit together so I at least have a cup of coffee to down amidst his emphatic cursing. He's very creative with his insults. They can be almost Shakespearean.

"Shit-eating maggots have more sense than these people do. They wouldn't know which end was up if they were part of the human centipede."

I see we're going more contemporary today. And so it goes. On. And on. And on.

THREE HOURS LATER, I collapse at my desk. At least

when I check my personal cell, there's a text from Rey:

Call me.

This is promising. I take a well-deserved minute to do just that, resting my feet on my desk.

"Aloha, kitten."

"Hawaii?"

"If you don't mind the flight."

"I don't."

"Good. I'll have Matthew make the arrangements."

"You're the best. Give Matty a kiss for me."

"Will do. We'll talk later."

I press the end call button on my phone and tuck it back into my purse. That's one thing I don't have to worry about anymore. Seventy-two hours of debauchery and my clock will be reset. I'll be good to go for another month or so. I take a deep breath and close my eyes before I press the intercom button.

"Lucy."

"More coffee, Ms. Burke?"

"Please."

It's going to be a long day.

TWELVE HOURS LATER, I'm on my way home and Jack's got a draft of the report on his desk. He'll hate it, but it's better to give him a product that needs a lot of work than to give him nothing at all. He's not difficult to manage once you understand him, but I think most of my predecessors—my many, *many* predecessors—were scared off before they had the chance.

Not me. I've got my sights set on running the place one day. Of course, I'll have to change the name. Jack Valentine Associates has a nice ring to it, but I think Burke Consulting Group sounds better. I'll get rid of the heavy wood and leather bank décor and go more airy and modern. But I've got a few years to plan my interior decorating. Jack's still got two kids in college from his second marriage. Or are they from his third? I can never keep track, although I know he's on wife number four. Candi—with an *i* that I bet the vacuous woman dots with a fucking heart. Thinking about her bottle-blonde head and unsubtle boob job make me cringe. There you have reasons number seventy-eight and seventy-nine why I'll never get married: becoming that or being left for that.

At any rate, I think I've got, at most, seven years before I'm in Jack's corner office. Which is reason number three: it's hard to sit behind that luxuriously big desk if you've got a husband and kids on the other end of your phone. I know people do it and do it well, but it can't be easy and it's not worth the bother to me. I didn't bust my ass at Princeton and Columbia to change diapers, oh no.

I spend the rest of my drive mentally redecorating Jack's office and selecting the color scheme for my business cards. By the time I've parked my car in the garage, stumbled into and out of the elevator, and made it down the endless hallway to my apartment, it's eleven thirty, and I debate whether or not to call Rey. After a minute of half-hearted agonizing while I kick off my shoes and hang my bag by the door, I dial. If he's busy, he'll let it go to voicemail, but it's rare he doesn't take my calls. Sometimes if he's in the middle of a training, but often even then.

"Kitten, I'm glad you called. I've been waiting on you."

"I hope not. I should've texted to say I'd be late. I'm sorry."

"No, no, I didn't mean it like that. I've been looking forward to talking, that's all. I think you're going to be very pleased."

"Hawaii's a good start. What else have you got for me?"

"Y'ever play with a Cris Ardmore?"

I pause for a second. "No. Would I know him by any other name?"

"Nope." I hear his smirk all the way from the Castro, and I know why. He knows it annoys me when people play with ridiculous fake names (e.g., Strider the Hobbit), which is pretty hypocritical but can't be helped. I have huge respect for anyone who plays with their real names. "He goes by Cris. No *h*."

My nose wrinkles.

"No *h*, huh?" The respect-o-meter has gone down. That's almost as bad as Candi with an *i*. Why no *h*? I shouldn't be too harsh. His parents could be dingbats, and I shouldn't fault the guy for that. God knows I'd get scrapped from just about anything if having sane parents were a requirement.

"Give the guy a break, India."

"You know me too well. Tell me more about this Cris Ardmore."

"He's on the big island, been active in the scene for a long time there and on the West Coast. I asked around—no one's got a bad thing to say about the guy. Safe player, knows the rules, keeps his subs happy."

"Why haven't I run into him before?"

Rey pauses, and I wonder if his hesitation is from reluctance or because he's so damned delighted with himself he wants to make a royal pronouncement.

"He's monogamous with his subs, and he just ended a five-year contract."

Holy. Shit.

"I get to be the rebound fuck?" I squeal with delight.

"Yes, you do."

"You're the best! How did you pull this off?"

"I know a guy."

"You know *all* the guys." I hold my phone to my ear with my shoulder as I pour the last of a bottle of Malbec into a glass. "But seriously, you're amazing. What do you want? I'll do anything."

He laughs. "Why don't you wait until you get back to sell your soul to the devil?"

"You're hardly the devil. I'm about to sing you the fucking Hallelujah chorus."

"And you'd sound like an angel, but we don't have time. Matthew is putting together a dossier for you. In the meantime, anything specific you want to know about the illustrious Mr. Ardmore?"

"How old is he?"

"Thirty-nine."

Well within my range.

"Do I get a picture?"

"You do."

"Is his contract weird?"

"I don't have it yet. He has to write one."

That's not unusual. Most of the guys Rey finds for me don't keep contracts like this on hand.

"Was he surprised to get your call?"

"They always are."

I snort. I know.

"You're the best thing that ever happened to me, Reyes Llewellyn Walter. I could kiss you on the mouth."

"Monday night. We'll see if you still want to kiss me or if we've moved on to the punching phase. For now, go change into that sexy lingerie I know you wear when I'm not there and get some beauty sleep. Don't want to be all puffy for—"

"Cris Ardmore," I breathe, my mouth caressing his name. The more I say it, the more I like it. I don't even notice the missing *h* much anymore. Yes, Mr. Cris Ardmore sounds promising.

A GOOD THING, too, because the rest of my week is a fucking misery. The report gets done well and on time, but not for the lack of everyone and their mother trying to fuck me over. Tuesday went a lot like this:

"Janis, I don't care who you have to screw to get those numbers. Hell, I don't care who *I* have to screw to get those numbers, but I need them by close of business, or we'll all be fucked and not in a nice way.

"Look, this is my job on the line, but it's your life. If this doesn't work out, they know it's not our fault and you're going to flat-out lose the units. They're going to take your funding away, Janis. Every penny. Is that how you want to go down in history?

"Every single motherfucking last housing authority is watching you and I would suggest not making any more of a hash out of this than you already have. Get me the goddamn vacancy numbers by the end of the day, or I'll make the call to Cooper myself."

I slam the receiver down and am surprised by a slow clap coming from my door.

"Well done, Ms. Burke. I didn't think you had it in you."

"You know I do, Jack. I just like to save it for special occasions, not wank off every day like you."

Thankfully, he laughs like I thought he would. I've caught him in a good mood. His hair's only slightly disheveled, and his tie's still on.

"What's up?" I ask, not bothering to take my feet off my desk.

Jack launches into concerns about some of the other projects we're working on. I take notes on things I need to take care of and issue assurances on what I've already dealt with. It's not the longest laundry list he's ever had for me, and everything should be taken care of by the time I leave.

He says on his way out, "You sure are earning that three-day weekend you talked me into."

"I always do."

"Yes, you do."

Though I technically only get two weeks of vacation per year, I've talked Jack into giving me three for all intents and purposes. He doesn't seem to care as long as it doesn't interfere with my projects. Not to mention he can see the difference when I get back. I'm more focused, more patient, work longer hours, and don't flinch no matter how harsh he is. All in all, well worth it for him.

I check my personal cell when he's gone, and there's another text from Rey:

LMK when you're home. I've got a messenger in a holding pattern.

Fun. This must be the dossier on Cris Ardmore. That will make for some interesting reading while I lounge in the tub with a glass of Pinot tonight. But first…

"Lucy!"

"Coffee?"

"Please."

This budget for the City of La Jolla is a certified disaster, and it needs to be dealt with before I can go home. I don't bother to start looking at the spreadsheets until Lucy delivers what may as well be manna from heaven. She might be incapable of anticipating my needs, but the woman makes a damn good cup of coffee. I take a sip and dive in, emerging seven hours later with my rank gym bag and my ubiquitous roller bag stuffed with my laptop, notes for tomorrow, and a draft of the LAHA report Jack will scream at me for the second he gets me on the phone.

I text Rey as soon as I get home, and ten minutes later, there's a hipster with gauged ears and too many tats at my door. I guess Rey really did have him in a holding pattern. I give him a bottle of water and a nice tip before I send him on his way, and then slip into my waiting tub and get some more info on Mr. Ardmore.

Name:	Ardmore, Crispin Michael
Aliases:	Crispin Ardmore, Cris Ardmore, ██████
DoB:	10/25/████
Sex:	M
SSN:	██████
License #:	██████
Marital Status:	Single
Address:	██████
Occupation:	██████
Employer:	██████
Education, High School:	██████
Education, Undergraduate:	██████
Education, Graduate:	██████
Education, Professional:	None
Criminal Record:	None
Bank Accounts:	██████
	██████
	██████

Credit Scores:	▋▋▋
Current Partner(s):	None
Past Partner(s):	▋▋▋▋▋▋
HIV Status:	Negative
STI Status:	Negative

A lot of it is redacted. Despite requiring the information, I don't want to see it. I do like proof that it's been collected, and I want Rey to have it as an insurance policy in case anything goes awry—or, really, to ensure nothing goes aslant in the first place. I rarely get refused, despite the invasive nature of the prerequisites I insist on, but maybe it's too strange an opportunity to pass up.

Imagine: You get a call out of the blue from a well-respected trainer you've almost certainly heard of, and if you haven't, someone you know has. He offers you a weekend of no-strings-attached play with a trained submissive provided you pass the screening process. She'll come to you, and should you choose to spend the weekend with her somewhere other than your home, all expenses will be taken care of. If it sounds pretty alluring, it's meant to.

I've never bothered to ask the men who say yes why

they agree, and by definition, I don't have the opportunity to ask the ones who say no. There's no contact with refusals, and they don't get a second chance.

Everything here is in order, as I expected. Rey doesn't waste my time. And there's a perfectly reasonable explanation for the lack of *h* in Cris. *Crispin*. I like it. A lot. Not Christopher, not Christian—Crispin. I wonder giddily if he can recite the St. Crispin's Day speech from *Henry V*. I'd best get this out of my system before embarrassing myself by asking when we meet.

I'm also pleased by the undergraduate and graduate degrees. Not that I haven't played with some very fine men with a high school diploma or less—and a PhD by no means guarantees a guy knows his way around a woman's body—but Rey knows I'm slutty for postgraduate degrees. He must've been clapping his hands like a little girl at recess when he put this together. Or really, when he read it over after Matty put it together. I tease myself by flipping through a few more mostly-blacked-out pages consisting of some references Mr. Ardmore provided, along with a couple Rey sought out before he even talked to the guy.

I hold my breath before flipping to the last page where his picture awaits. When I get photos—and I don't always since I don't require it—they're usually full-body shots—although, mercifully, clothed. Believe it or not, Rey has to specify this. *Dude, we'll get there.* If it's not a head-to-toe, it's what looks like a professional head-shot. But this… It's a candid of a man. Laughing.

What? Usually they do their best to look intimidating, intense. You know, *dominating*. But not this guy. You can't even see his whole face because he's turned to the side, and he's *laughing*. The corner of my mouth tugs up involuntarily.

What's your game, Cris Ardmore?

He's got a mop of curly dark hair, what some might call bushy eyebrows but I don't mind, and a layer of what I'm hoping is perma-stubble. His teeth are white, straight and sharp against his tanned skin, and he's got what I think are light blue eyes. Or maybe grey. The picture isn't taken from close enough to say for sure.

I don't know if he'd be considered conventionally attractive—there's something off there—but I won't kick him out of bed. If I have the chance. Sleeping arrangements can be sticky with what I do. I won't fret about that now.

I grab my phone from where it's resting next to my empty wine glass and text Rey, despite it being almost one in the morning:

Me likey.

My phone pings a minute later:

Thought you would. Now go the fuck to sleep.

I laugh, text back a kiss, and do as I'm told. I have an early morning tomorrow and don't even have Adam's puppy-dog face to look forward to.

Despite being wrecked and having had one—okay,

three—glasses of wine, I have trouble falling asleep. I find myself wondering if I'll get to see Cris Ardmore laugh. I think I'd like to.

To continue reading Cris and India's story, please visit
http://tamsenparker.com/personal-geography/
for purchase options. Thank you for reading!

Made in the USA
Middletown, DE
30 October 2015